Praise for A Carnival of Atr

"What an event! Natalia Garc
ancient forest and sets langu
including the living and dead. Marvelous, dazzling,
celebratory writing. I can't say it enough: read it!"
MARÍA SÁNCHEZ

"The language in this novel weaves together miracles,
curses and deliriums. Natalia García Freire creates
disturbing and beautiful books that make us think of the
poetic cruelty of far-off mythologies."
IRENE VALLEJO

"This is the story of a town, Cocuán, told through its
characters. A story with hints of fable, myth, madness,
death, innocence, evil ... It's amazing, as always."
ANDREA CARRASCO, *ABC*

"*A Carnival of Atrocities*, the story of poor Mildred,
banished, dispossessed, and ostracized, is
preserved in Mother Earth, Pachamama, in Cocuán."
INÉS GARCÍA, *Libero Editorial*

"In Natalia García Freire's literary universe everything
that was destined to remain a secret, hidden away,
has come to light: the wind, the birds, the forest. She
writes from the ground level, somewhere between the
ferocity of Flannery O'Connor and the sinister nature
of Shirley Jackson—it will leave no one indifferent.
Hers is a mad and disturbing universe."
CRISTINA SÁNCHEZ ANDRADE

"A beautiful and terrible book."
JOSEP NADAL SUAU

●

Praise for This World Does Not Belong to Us

"Disquieting and visceral ... García Freire unearths a brilliant sense of the miraculous from the swarming and putrid subject matter. The result is beautifully macabre."
Publishers Weekly, starred review

"One of the debut novels that most stood out this year in Latin America."
New York Times

"A wronged, bitter young man welcomes his fate in Natalia García Freire's novel *This World Does Not Belong to Us*. Lucas was just a child when his father sold him to another farmer as a laborer. Years later, Lucas returns, full of resentment and burning for revenge ... Visceral prose captures Lucas's obsession with death, bugs, and other unpleasant aspects of life ... There is a strange, unconventional beauty to his morbid world—a beauty that helps him endure pain and humiliation and achieve an unnerving final calm. *This World Does Not Belong to Us* is a bleak exploration of how all ends in death and decay."
Foreword Reviews

"A deliciously menacing read which I just couldn't put down. Every word punches hard. *This World Does Not Belong to Us* treads the fine line between beauty and horror effortlessly."
JAN CARSON, author of *The Raptures*

A Carnival of Atrocities

NATALIA GARCÍA FREIRE

A Carnival of Atrocities

Translated from the Spanish
by Victor Meadowcroft

WORLD EDITIONS
New York

Published in the USA in 2025 by World Editions NY LLC, New York

World Editions
New York

Copyright © Natalia García Freire, 2022
Original title Trajiste Contigo El Viento
First published in 2022 by La Navaja Suiza
Published by arrangement with CASANOVAS & LYNCH
LITERARY AGENCY S.L.

English translation copyright © Victor Meadowcroft, 2025
Cover illustrations © Annemarie van Haeringen
Author portrait © María García Freire
Interior images © Natalia García Freire

Printed by Lightning Source, USA

Library of Congress Cataloging in Publication Data is available

ISBN 978-1-64286-151-8

Company: worldeditions.org
Facebook: @WorldEditionsInternationalPublishing
Instagram: @WorldEdBooks
TikTok: @worldeditions_tok
Twitter: @WorldEdBooks
YouTube: World Editions

For those who are missing, Maita and Diego;
for Gabriela and mamá, who
won't let me forget them,
and for Seydú, who, on seeing a flower,
cries viva, viva!

The voice said it resembled a novel written against
history, a novel close to the end of history
and written in a jungle clearing: written where
a civilization is born and dies or where the last
survivor of a civilization meditates with the
barbarians breathing in his ear,
unaware that the barbarian is him.

GUSTAVO FAVERÓN PARTIAU, *Vivir abajo* (Living Below)

Sometimes nature plays tricks on us
and we imagine we are something
other than what we truly are.
Is this a key to life in general?
Or the case of the two-headed schizophrenic?
Both heads thought the other
was following itself.
Finally, when one head wasn't looking,
the other shot the other right between the eyes,
and, of course, killed himself.

LOG LADY, *Twin Peaks*

Do not long for the night,
when people vanish in their places.

JOB, 36:20

THE PROPHECY OF MILDRED CAPA

Remember this, Mildred, remember it well, ma told me before she died:

Don't scratch yourself. Clean your ass and your pee-hole properly, go out onto the balcony every day until you feel like snuffing out the sun. Wash your clothes every day, wash them twice; as soon as they wear out, burn them. And don't ever let anyone see your sores.

Then she closed her eyes. Her eyelids quivered for a moment. Pa lifted the sheet off her and showed me her body, which was no longer dark-skinned, but had turned a milky white, the substance cold is made of. Her breasts were very small, like mine, her ribs stuck out like those of a crucified Christ and her pubis was covered in thick black hair.

Look at your ma, he said. Look at her now she's closed her eyes to us and opened them to the heavens. And then he took a hammer to the door, which had loose hinges and would scrape the wooden floor with a sound like grinding teeth in a tight jaw.

From time to time, pa talked to me.

Mildred, listen, Mildred. When you were born your ma said you brought the wind with you. It was a tepid wind, a wind that isn't scared, a wind that takes refuge among piles of hay and rests down wells, emerging later to softly touch the flowers and make them open, before filtering through the tunnels in leaves where it remembers that it's wind because it whistles. You brought the wind with you, the one that carries dandelion puffs all over the world, Mildred. The wind that soothes the livestock. That wind isn't scared. Those who live in fear will become savages. But not you, listen to me, Mildred, not you. Your ma would touch your sored skin and smile, because she said beneath it you were full of light. They've sent us an angel, she told me when we brought you to the river so you could be blessed by the water, we'll call her Mildred, and we'll never let them take her away. And the wind that year caused the waters to recede, Mildred, and it brought thrushes and turtledoves and swallows. And it was that same wind that swept away the cochineals, the fleas, the aphids and the whiteflies.

When pa had finished, he tested the door a couple of times and calmly walked outside.

Stay here, inside our house, Mildred, and watch over your ma, he said.

Hammer in hand, he disappeared between the stakes that marked the boundary of our land. I watched him leave from the bedroom window and remained standing there by ma's body, which had turned cold and gray.

Fireflies and cicadas brought the sound of night, ma's eyes sank into their sockets, her stomach swollen like that of a fat doll, and pa did not come back.

The parish priest, Father Santamaría, arrived and found me standing there, the white sheet lying on the floor, soiled by a liquid oozing from ma's body. He took her away wrapped in blankets. I tried to stop him, but he held me off with one hand, touching an area of my chest with sores on it. I trembled.

Tell your father we'll hold vigil for just one day, then tomorrow we'll have the funeral.

The house grew dark, the wind blew hard and I fell asleep and dreamed of ma turned into a fat doll that kept shrinking until it was the size of a fingernail, and then disappeared, transformed into particles of dust and light.

Pa did not come back for the funeral.

I couldn't travel into town, even though ma's body was there, I just couldn't. I went to the porch and pulled the peonies she loved up from the ground and put on a dress that was the same pale blue as the sky during the unseasonably warm days of the veranillo del niño. It was the dress ma liked best, and I walked along the river path, flowers in hand like a bride, hopping, skipping.

Then I sat down and cried.

I was tired and the flowers had withered. Night fell and I could feel my sores burning. I lifted my dress and caressed their shapes with my fingertips, as ma had always done. Sometimes I imagined I had a tiny sun inside me, which burned, leaving the surface of my skin covered in stars, clusters and galaxies. Then I would think that my skin communicated in the language of light, but I couldn't understand it, because that language must be as old as the first specters that roamed the earth, instilling visions in humans and sending chills down their spines.

There was an echo coming from the town, the murmur of singing. Down there they always sang the same thing when someone died: Darkness be over me, my rest a stone, Yet in my dreams I'd be nearer, my God, to thee. I wasn't sure why they were singing at ma's funeral, it isn't as though they knew her well; they never came up to the house and she didn't go into town except to pay Old Iván for the land. Ma hated Cocuán.

When I got back home, pa still hadn't returned, his boots weren't on the landing, nor his hat on the table. I went inside and caught a whiff of bleach and menthol behind me. When I turned around, I saw Father Santamaría standing in the doorway, darkened by the night. I was afraid of his blue eyes, his small mouth and that freckled skin which so resembled that of a child.

We buried your mother today, he said. She's in the cemetery. You must at least go down and lay a flower.

Ma didn't let me go into town, I said.

Your ma isn't here anymore. The townsfolk and I believe you would be better off down in one of the houses or at the monastery.

I didn't reply and quickly tried to push the door shut, but the parish priest jammed his foot in. He pulled my sleeve hard. The neckline of my dress came open and I caught him looking at my sores.

Don't be so stubborn, he told me.

Pa will be back soon, I replied.

I took hold of his arm with my trembling hands, moved a little closer, then turned my face up and spat at him.

I'll come see you again tomorrow, Mildred.

The next day, I fed beets to the donkeys, changed the bucket of water, washed my clothes and took the pigs out to graze. Then I led them to the river and sank into the water with them. All around, tall sharp leaves of grass encircled us. And the pigs were so happy that they clambered out to lie down in the grass, flattening it with their round bodies, before coming back to cool their skin, thick like mine. Sometimes, I would float face-down, trying to see what lived at the bottom of the river, but I only ever managed to spot the occasional carp, hugging the curve of the riverbend.

When I emerged from the water, the sun was pouring down over the entire forest. The pigs had fallen asleep. I woke them with soft taps on the ears and led them home. I named them Ramón, Eustabio, and Lupe, who was the noisiest of the lot. Lupe, I would yell at her, quit moaning like an old busybody, and then she'd go quiet for a moment and come nuzzle my legs with her damp snout and I'd laugh. I laid down large beds of hay for them in the kitchen. That night, I slept with the pigs and discovered that hay keeps warmth underneath. Two cold snouts nuzzled my neck and Ramón rested his head on my belly. It was as heavy as a fig-leaf gourd. They slept peacefully and kept me good company.

It was the pigs that woke up first. They rubbed their snouts against my face so I'd give them something to eat. They had the same heavy breath as pa and ma did in the morning. We shared some fruit and plants from the vegetable garden and they followed me wherever I went. They played with the donkeys using an old ball pa kept in his bedroom, wallowed in puddles and looked up at the sky when thrushes passed over, while I split pea pods to make a stew for lunch.

When we grew bored, we went into the kitchen to roll around in the hay, and the pigs made the sound of baby ferrets.

That day, the priest came by and left me some holy water.

Apply it to your sores, he told me, and leave the pigs outside.

I showed him how they played in the hay and told him to listen to the little ferret sounds they made, but he didn't know how to look or listen. He went silent and turned his head the other way. He told me to go with him, that he would take me in at the monastery.

No, I said, pa asked me to stay here.

Tomorrow I'll come for you, Mildred, he repeated.

And he continued to return for many days, and I would tell him: Pa is coming back.

But he didn't know how to listen. He would just go silent and look the other way. He returned one Saturday with the Solina sisters, who gave me a knitted dress and brought cheese empanadas with panela syrup. I opened the door just wide enough to receive the packages. I didn't let them in the house. And they came back in the evening, now accompanied by Old Iván, the person who leased the lands to pa and ma. This second time, I did have to open the door, but I didn't offer them anything. Ramón, who spent his afternoons watching the apple trees from an armchair, scampered over to hide behind my legs. It wasn't true the house smelled of stale drain water. They were the ones who brought the smell with them.

You can no longer farm these lands, said Old Iván.

I'm old enough to do it, I replied.

The Father has told us about your illness.

Pa is coming back, I said.

Warily, I covered up my neck. I got up and stood by the door. There was nothing I could say, but I wanted them to go. They took the hint and left.

But they came back.

They always came back. They brought more men from town. They measured out the land, pulled up the stakes of the enclosure and led the donkeys from the stable. Our donkeys went slouching after Germán and Abdiel. Whenever the men came to bang on our door, I would open it without releasing the chain. I repeated that pa was coming back, that it was only a matter of days until his return, and they would leave us alone for a day or two. Later, they came back. They also came back on Monday and Tuesday and Saturday, and there wasn't a single day I didn't fear that one of them would get in while I slept.

It was a full-moon night when I heard them coming up between the hills and saw them crossing the vegetable garden. They were advancing in procession. A swarm of sleepwalking hearts, smelling of milk, of stagnant water, a dense and peculiar mix. Pigs don't smell like we do, of rotten milk. They smell of thick hide and newly cut pastures, of fresh grass and rain. The women of Cocuán would mask their scent with perfumed talcs they bought by the kilo at the town pharmacy. I used to watch them as a young girl, when ma let me go with her into town. Before she forbade me from ever accompanying her again. Behind the women came the men who smelled of cheap Franja Negra cologne, which they purchased in blue glass bottles. Ma only ever used that cologne for curing wounds and headaches, because the fragrance reminded her of them, and ma loathed the men of Cocuán. I was also driven mad by that smell, which grew stronger as they drew nearer.

I shut all the doors and windows and Ramón hid beneath the table. Lupe went silent.

May all the gods curse you, may the heavens and the earth curse you, I said out loud, with my hands and jaw clenched. I didn't stop repeating it. It was an old curse ma used all the time: when Old Iván raised the price of the land, when the parish priest tried to force her to have me baptized, when Esther left leaflets with prayers to the Virgin Mary, telling her to copy them forty times and hand them out in order to ward off tragedy. Ma paid no attention and cursed them all.

The tide of men and women was coming ever closer. It was midnight. The bell in the town chapel tolled twelve times. The moon lit up several wrinkled scalps, then its brightness went and hid among the leaves of ivy and lady-of-the-night that covered the front walls of our house.

They arrived with their hearts all aflutter. I could almost hear them beating, speeding up as they drew nearer. It wasn't their custom to come out at midnight. They were scared of the dark forest, scared of the animals. They were scared of everything. The people of Cocuán came and went with the sun. They were like starlings that returned from the fields to their roosts at night, hiding their heads under their wings and sleeping a shared sleep.

But they were coming closer to our house, the house belonging to ma and pa and me. The house where ma had turned gray and where her sunken eyes had closed their lids to avoid attracting crows. The house where I was born and where pa would paint the walls, covering them in flowers and clouds during the month of November when the rains didn't come.

They drew nearer, brushing past the flowers of my lady-of-the-night, lit up like stars by the moonlight. I spied on them from behind the curtain, which was pale blue like the dress ma gave me, like the sky during the veranillo del niño. From a distance, I was able to see little Berta Sotelo, covering her scars with the long widow's dress her mother made her wear. Poor Berta, I thought, her mother had dropped her into a rose bush. The doctor refused to remove even a single thorn. Days later, she became filled with pus and expelled the thorns like someone giving birth to hundreds of prickly children. Poor Berta. Her mother never took proper care of her. She was ashamed of her. I knew all this from what ma had told me. I also saw Jonás, who was wearing a tattered shirt, his pants in need of ironing. When he reached the lady-of-the-night, he turned tail and ran until he disappeared. They weren't all bad. And I didn't want to, but inside I couldn't keep myself from cursing them, all of them. There were also other children I didn't recognize. They snaked between the stiff legs, kicked stones on the path and shook the bougainvillea branches until a tug on the forearm quietened them down. I saw Old Iván and Abdiel. And then I saw nothing more, because they had come to a sudden halt. The tide of men, women and children stood rooted very close to the door of our house. I closed my eyes and prayed to ma.

Come out of there, Mildred, they said.

You can't keep living there, they cried.

We have to shut you away until your sores have healed.

I could hear the heavy pounding of my heart, and of Ramón's, Eustabio's and Lupe's. Then they started banging on the door, the one pa had taken a hammer to before he left. And the door shook, its hinges coming loose once more. All four of us were hiding beneath the table, surrounded by piles of hay, like a barricade about to be toppled by the wind.

Once they'd got the door open, Hermosina chased my pigs away with kicks. Mercedes and Esther ran to throw open the shutters.

We need to let some air in first, they said.

Between them, Abdiel, Old Iván, his son Baltasar, and Germán carried me out kicking, with the clothes— the ones ma had told me to burn—torn to shreds. And the women and children took the knitted fabrics out of ma's bedroom and took the crucifixes from the living room where pa used to mend old furniture while ma combed my hair with rosemary water.

This must be saved, they said.

And they removed all this and more, stuffing it into bags they carried far from the house. It was the parish priest who lit the flame, and the first thing to burn was the hay. They left me lying among the honey-suckles while our house was swallowed by the blaze. Ramón, Lupe and Eustabio hurried over to me. They no longer made the sound of little ferrets, but squealed now as the smoke reddened their eyes.

Their damp snouts brushed my neck, my chest, my hands. And their eyes squeezed shut, turning into fish eyes.

And I saw nothing more.

As if on the river, I was rocked, but did not feel the water. I was cradled by nothing but a white energy, waves with no sea. The men's voices and the smell of burning were getting further away, and again I saw ma's body, white like the cold, her pubis covered in thick black hair, the tunnel I had arrived through bringing the wind.

But that night there was no wind.

Suddenly, I saw a lot of light. I had never seen so much before. I didn't want to see it. So much light attracts flies and, later, nothingness. I felt a pain at the back of my eyes, but I could no longer hear the voices. Or smell the smoke.

The light began transforming into a forest of tall pines with sharp branches and rotted trunks, surrounded by stakes, the ground covered in prickly red pine needles and walled in by huge rocks. The whole of Cocuán was there. And they were singing. It was a terrifying song, as if the trees of seven mountains were crashing down, with the animals shrieking as they tried to escape beneath the trunks. They sang and I wanted to hear Ramón and Eustabio and Lupe, wanted to look for them, wanted to look for ma, but their song wouldn't let me.

Then they called me by my name.

The whole of Cocuán continued to sing, but other voices, the voices of a man, woman and child said:

Mildred.

Sweet and powerful Mildred.

Those who live in fear will become savages.

Look at them, they said. And the voices swelled like the high tide, the waves crashing into my ears. Look at them in their Sunday finest, huddled so close together. Look at them, Mildred, deaf to the wind and blind like corrupted animals. With the wills of slaves. Look at the men and women created by the Word, molded from the dust of dead stars. Look at their body, which is the body of Christ, and look at their disoriented eyes, their old bones on the brink of snapping. Look upon the town of God that has abandoned you. Look upon the town of God that you have cursed.

The whole of Cocuán continued to sing, pressing their lips together. Some of them raised their hands, their eyes clouded over, covered in a white shroud. They tried to flee, but were unable to. The rest kept them there, forcing them to sing. A town is a chain formed of nightmares.

The voices named them, one by one, and everyone in the town stood still. The voices began to howl and I did too. I howled loudly until my rage became an animal noise for cursing, an animal noise for condemning. They came nearer, then the rows of the choir dispersed without ceasing their singing, and they tore at their clean clothes until they were left naked. They wrenched up the wooden stakes from the ground with both hands and buried them into one another as they continued to give voice to that song of dead animals.

Living flesh is very wicked! they screamed.

They screamed and laughed.

Screamed and cried.

And then they beat one another, scratched one another, wounded one another fatally, and their blood, which was thick, seeped into the tall grass, staining my lady-of-the-night, which began to grow and surround their bodies, in tight spirals, drawing them into a death that was white

green

white.

Those who live in fear will become savages, said all the voices in unison.

And I felt the warm wind that caused the waters to

recede, that carried the flies and aphids far away, and I heard the song of the thrushes and saw an eagle screech and soar over the edge of the forest, now lined with naked bodies with quivering eyes, all enveloped in lady-of-the-night.

Spirals of never-ending death.

And the voices continued to talk in a language I could no longer understand.

I awoke inside the monastery, my entire body covered in a black cassock that rubbed my sores. It prickled and stung.

In the mornings, Father Santamaría would hear my confession, and on seeing that I did not speak, he became irritated; and every morning he would read to me from the Bible, and on seeing that I did not listen, he became irritated; and every morning he would leave me jellied pigeon and rye bread, and on seeing that I did not eat, he became irritated. Sometimes, I was visited at the monastery by a girl covered in birds, and a woman with mountains on her back. But the parish priest would banish them. He didn't want anyone to see me. He dabbed holy water on my skin, but my sores only grew larger. And they shone. I would touch them as ma had done, until he tied my hands together. He also killed my pigs—Lupe, Ramón and Eustabio.

Mildred, he would call to me, but it wasn't the voice of ma or pa, nor those other voices, those echoes of light that said, Sweet and powerful Mildred. Mildred, the parish priest would shout at me. And I howled. Mildred, he would beat and curse me. And I howled. Mildred, he shook and bruised me. Mildred, he would take me in the night and then spit on me. And my name became a hollow whisper, a wind of stale air that doesn't whistle.

All of this is in the past.

EZEQUIEL

There was a time when I'd set out to be a magnificent boy. I looked at the world with the palms of my hands, understood the language of reliefs, the vibration of colors, the gravity of forms; this is how I discovered a world that was beautiful and simple, like the plowed fields that wind across hillsides and from a distance look like paintings. This is how I experienced the world, and I may even have loved it. I didn't want it to end, which is why I went around with bandages over my eyes. I was seven years old and mamá could not stop laughing. She thought what I was doing was a game and didn't scold me when I knocked over glasses and flowerpots, simply fetching the broom and sweeping up the pieces. At that time, I used to pray as well. I prayed to everything, to the oldest eucalyptus tree down by the river, to the best egg-laying hen, to mamá's left breast, which was larger, and to an old cat that limped and seemed so all alone. But father had no patience with me, he just thrashed me. And I continued to search for a way to avoid seeing what I saw.

Of course, in the end, I gave up.

Maybe this was because what father said was true: I'm feebleminded. I removed the bandages and returned to my world of fury. There, instead of words, I saw a language composed of animal heads which bled and left red trails in their wake. If I looked up at the sky, the sun was always mid-explosion, and when I looked in a mirror, I could quite clearly see through my skull to a brain like a demented labyrinth in which burning men and headless women were always running about.

My eyes were Avernus, the entrance to the underworld.

I would always see Víctor as a mutilated child, with the bleeding heart of Christ and a serpent like the one from Eden slithering up his butt; mamá was a bichito, a creepy-crawly, dark and plump like a leach, and father was a man full of tumors and fat growths on his legs and cheeks that became even longer at his groin.

But not on that day. On the day father left, he looked different. He was no longer that elephant man with the innocent gaze of a child that drove me out of my mind. The day he vanished, his body looked immaculate to me, shiny, with perfect hands. It made you wish he would touch your brow and bless you.

Where are you going so early, father? I asked him that morning.

But he didn't answer, merely stood before me, very close. My forehead grazed his chest and he began to howl. I felt a shiver run through me and wanted to ask what the hell was wrong with him, when he covered his ears as if something had ruptured deep inside him. Then he started babbling, and that's how he left, with his hands over his ears, his pants falling down, ass half hanging out, and walking slowly, bathed in light. A blessed fool among the wilderness.

The old man did not return that day. Mamá was convinced he'd gone out drinking. He'll be back, she proclaimed, with mussed-up hair and his suit all covered in aguardiente and filth. Yet I knew he wouldn't. Although it's true the old man would often leave without saying anything, returning drunk a few days later and going straight to bed, which mamá lined with black plastic bags in case he pissed in his sleep.

That day, however, there was something different and I knew it, I was sure the old man wasn't coming back.

In the early hours of the morning, Mamá Bichito finally fell asleep, but Víctor said it wasn't right to leave the old man out there for so long, wherever he was, no matter how drunk he might be. Víctor-Heart-of-Christ was always coming up with big ideas for saving the world, he wanted to save souls and wasn't satisfied with the little pigeon souls in matchboxes I brought him as offerings, before which he would break down in tears. Víctor would never give in when it came to father, so we went out looking for him.

We left mamá snoring on the chair in the kitchen, which was filled with steam coming from an old pot where some turnips and carrots were simmering. Mamá Bichito slept and cooked all day and night and smelled of stale sleep and grime.

We took the old rifles father kept in the cellar—from the time when he used to run guns for grandfather—as well as a couple of black-spotted bananas, and set off in silence. For half the journey, I sat in the handcart while Víctor pulled, then we swapped over and I pulled as he stood scanning from side to side, hand at his brow like a sailor. It was just like the time we saw the wolf. The first impression you have when you see a wolf is good, something beautiful and gray is happening to you. It's only later you realize that the wolf is coming for you. That's how it was with the old man. In the beginning it was a real adventure.

> Death is just like a pirate,
> It eats tough meat and drinks salt water.
> Death is just like a pirate,
> It bares its ass, then goes for the slaughter.

This is what we sang on the way to the waterfall where Víctor believed the old man might have gone, because several times before we had found him teetering there, with his eyes closed, covered by the water, and been forced to drag him back to the house like a stuffed dummy I would have liked to watch burn on an enormous bonfire fed with ragweed and rue to chase away the old man's evil spirit, the fleas and the flies. But no one wanted to hear my dirty plans, least of all Víctor, who loved the old man with a stupid love. So that's where we were headed, once again, to look for him.

Before reaching the waterfall, we came to the forest of frailejones. Day was breaking, and as I stood there, submerged in the jubilance of the tussock grass, with the first rays of sunlight, I managed to get Víctor to forget about father for a minute.

That's the Judases' ranch, you'll have to cross through there, said Víctor.

He said this with his hands at his waist and the grown-up voice of a cowboy, like when our games turned serious.

I've been this way before, bastard, I'm familiar with the Judases, I told him, they won't let us through, they'd sooner kill us.

You'll go for my cattle.

Forget it.

That's when I took one of the rifles from the handcart. It was rusted and grimy, but gripping it gave you an urge to do evil. Víctor came over and sent the gun flying with a kick. He grabbed the remaining rifle and the bang-bang of our brawl filled the entire forest and the morning, until we came together, gasping, face-to-face, dragging ourselves along like lizards, unsure exactly when the game had ended. We lay there in the grass, bruised and sweaty, allowing our weapons to fall.

And what if the old man doesn't come back? asked Víctor.

It'll be a kind of liberation, I told him, I know that Judas, one of these days he'll end up killing us.

In the distance, we heard the barking of the dogs.

Damn it, said Víctor, slapping his forehead, we didn't put anything down for Mucky.

Mucky is our dog. We feed him, but he lives with the other dogs at the dump; they roam freely, and on afternoons they come up here in a pack to hunt foxes. They dive into the wilderness, only pausing to scratch themselves, because they're always covered in ticks and fleas. They bury their cold noses in the damp earth, in the mire, in fields of violets and nettles, in hailstones, straw or excrement, and then, as if having a collective epiphany, they all raise their snouts and charge off with the absolute conviction they're going to catch them. But they never do, they're dumb and scrawny. They might perhaps be able to hunt some bird, but that doesn't interest them in the slightest. They're obsessed with foxes. Mucky isn't one of the brighter ones, he sometimes pisses in his sleep, but he's our dog.

I asked Víctor if we should go back for Mucky. If it was up to me, we would. I wanted to run back in search of our Mucky, head through town with the old rifle in hand and give those Solina sisters a couple of sharp raps on the ankles with the buttstock. We wouldn't get another chance. Those Solina sisters only showed their faces during the days of the veranillo, and they grew fatter with each appearance. I was convinced it wouldn't be long before they burst and died. The rest of the year I imagined them sleeping inside enormous sarcophaguses where their flesh swelled up like rotting corpses. Each of them had three extra chins. But during the veranillo they would come out and sit on that filthy iron bench they had outside their house. They crocheted as their cats chased the balls of yarn, tangling them up until one of the sisters, sometimes Esther, sometimes Mercedes, sometimes Hermosina, planted some hard kicks on the kittycats, one by one, right on the jaw, and they scurried off to take refuge under the old boards of the porch, with the Solina sisters continuing to knit those little cardigans for Zaida and Chabuca, their daughters, who were surely skinny because they were denied food, and they would carry on taking in the sunshine and cultivating jowls of flesh and filth. They deserved to have their ankles rapped until their souls bruised. But Víctor didn't want to, Víctor-Heart-of-Christ wanted us to waste our time looking for the old man, wanted to find him and weep with him, because of him, for him.

He picked up the guns, tied the handcart to a pine tree and started walking back toward the path from which we'd strayed at dawn.

He's going to kill himself, I said.

Víctor didn't answer.

He's going to kill himself. Father's going to hell, mamá is too. And you and I can go far away if we forget about them.

Víctor kept advancing slowly, delving between the ragged branches, his tattered shoes of an abandoned child crushing turnip flowers, yellow like those of a bouquet, and nettles, mint, fresh grass. And me, behind him, playing his game. Like the dogs of Cocuán I went sniffing the air as if transfixed, searching for the old man, while the old man—who can say? Perhaps he was hiding in some vast crater of earth, laughing wildly, white flecks of saliva flying from his mouth, like the bald, deformed and malicious drunk that he was.

We could have a good life, Víctor. If you weren't so set on saving their skins, we'd be unstoppable.

Do you ever plan to give me any peace?

Víctor is good like a Samaritan, but if you ever mention the word dick around him, he turns into a nasty ogre.

I shouldn't have said it, but I wanted to go back, and Víctor just carried on walking with his long shadow, as though he'd had to drag it up the mountain. He hurried off down that path inhabited by evening mist and lit by the faint light that penetrated the forest. Víctor was becoming ever smaller, as though returning to his childhood. I almost lost sight of him and—my god!—I shouldn't have followed his trail, because by the time I caught up with him, he'd become a little shrimp, as small as when he was born and just as wrinkled. He was at the base of the waterfall. He brushed his sleeve across his sweaty face, his eyes red and his throat quivering: he was holding back tears.

Kneeling in the saw-sedge and tule rushes, pulling them up like weeds, he placed his hand over his heart and started bawling and talking—both things at once, the words falling like fat droplets formed in his eyes. I could barely hear what he said due to the force of the water crashing behind him.

Just help me find him. That's all. I won't ask you for anything else, he screamed.

That's what you and mamá always say, but the pair of you get off on all this. You're as dumb as she is. You both love chasing after that stinky old man. It's almost like you're begging him to beat you and abandon you.

It was all Víctor's fault. Because just seeing him was enough to make me feel sick to my bones, I wanted to break myself apart inside, wanted my very blood to go stiff and shatter like ice, destroying me from the inside out. I pitied that brother of mine, limp-armed and lame, unable to live outside the shit, but my blood continued to course all around my body, liquid and black, causing my temples and sex to throb, because like the old man said, I'm feebleminded and damaged inside. And there are no bandages that could cover what I saw there, within the demented labyrinth of my mind.

Víctor went quiet and touched his eyelids with his fingertips; he knelt down, his back to the light and the crag behind him, as the sun was extinguished and night fell over him, inside him. I approached slowly, with the stealth of a deer, and held out my hand.

When he raised his head, I gazed at him with tenderness. In that moment, I wanted to store all the luster in those eyes of a crucified Christ alongside my world of plowed hillsides.

So I did.

That's when I started hitting him. Víctor covered his face and I kept pounding my fists into the bones of his arms, his ribs, as if I were an avenger, and if I'd had a real gun, I would have blown his brains out, but I didn't, so I kept hitting him. I pulled off those pitiful shoes of an abandoned child and beat him with them too, and Víctor continued to cover his face, not defending himself, weeping like when he saw the little pigeon souls in the matchboxes, dusky and frail, like kittens born lame and blind; I also removed his pants and his underwear and peed over him, and I could swear that he enjoyed it, as much as Mamá Bichito, who turned bright red when father beat her. One time, she made us toss the aguardiente that the old man would hide straight into a fire that soon grew enormous, and around which we all leaped and danced, waving our hands, swatting away the smoke that gave shape to the air, and when the old man arrived, he first thrashed us and then went to see her in the kitchen, dragging her out into the garden by her matted hair and beating her there until, half-broken, Mamá Bichito began to laugh out loud.

After a while, I grew tired of hearing Víctor's sobs and his body became a mushy thing I no longer wished to hit, so I took off into the dark forest.

I removed my boots and carried on barefoot, my heels all calloused, because I hated when mamá took the pumice stone to them. There were only bushes, old pear trees, clumps of tussock grass and large, moss-covered rocks. The wind was fearsome, branches sprang out right in front of me, there was the noise of frogs and cicadas—as well as silhouettes or shadows and shivers made of spiderweb that grazed my arms and cheeks—until I heard the quiet rustle of dry leaves, as if someone had been following me; I turned and went as rigid as a tree trunk.

A reddish fox appeared from behind a pear tree, looking at me and remaining hunched and still, with two very small pups behind her. She was staring straight at me, directly into my eyes, not moving. Her gaze was cunning and delirious. I was left stunned as a moth, and she just stood there, defiant, some thirty feet away. She was waiting for me to leave, but I couldn't move, that dirty fox's gaze had me bewitched.

To begin with, I didn't want to, I mean, the idea just crossed my mind, but soon it was as if my head filled up with broken radios, pure white noise. I picked up a sharp stone, without taking my eyes off her, and threw it as hard as I could. Not toward her; I threw it at one of the pups. The fox snatched up the other pup in its jaws and scampered off. The one I'd struck ran too, but slowly and clumsily. My stone had hit its mark. I went over and found him cowering behind a rock. I picked him up and stroked him the way I stroke Mucky. His heart was beating very fast, he moved a hind leg to dislodge my hand and tried to brush my neck with his head. He couldn't decide whether to escape or stay with me so I could care for him. I thought how his heart wouldn't be small enough to fit inside a matchbox.

It was like breaking a chicken's neck. Before the snap he squeaked like a weasel and the smell he released was pungent, like rabbit's urine.

I looked behind me and realized I was very near to the crag. I would need to move away from there, walk in the opposite direction, if I wished to leave the forest. I strode calmly toward the path, passing through the tussock grass that had brought us such pleasure that morning. I thought of my father, of how he had left the house with that bright light that seemed to pass through him, and gone off so peacefully, as if he were someone else. That old baldy would pay. From the time I was small, I'd been sure there would come a day when my father would shrink like all old people do and be left hunched forever in the rocking chair, and then we would leave him to scrabble around in his own shit, or feed him like a prisoner, sliding his food back and forth, before launching it through the air, dying from laughter. I came up with all kinds of torture scenarios. But I already suspected things wouldn't turn out that way, that father had devised some plan to spare himself that ending, that ultimately we would be the ones left paying for the rest of our lives; Víctor and I would kill each other, while Mamá Bichito and father wouldn't even be upset, they'd continue to live amid blows and sobs and yelps and let the party roll on.

The fox's pelt was so soft I would have liked to wear it around my neck, but then I'd smell of fox for the rest of my life. I kept walking toward the forest entrance by Old Mildred's house. Some of the townsfolk said the old woman would appear to you engulfed in the curse of fire; when going past her home, they would cross themselves, and every month Father Manzi sprinkled holy water around what had once been the house and in the river that ran behind it. It was rumored Father Santamaría had gone mad because of her. But no one wanted to tell us the details of that story, and Mamá Bichito would cover our ears whenever they mentioned her. All you could see in that place was tree trunks, rotten stakes and the little that was left of the brick walls. I entered with the fox in my hand. Then I noticed the smell, different to the rest of Cocuán, which reeked of dirty water and grime. By Old Mildred's house, it smelled of fresh grass and rain. I had never been inside. Only the pigs went in to roll in the honeysuckles and black-eyed Susan vines, which grew quickly and covered the old walls, like the ruins of another world. I remained in that place for a long time, because it was soothing, like when someone strokes the back of your neck. I heard the barking of the dogs, and then they all arrived together, as usual. Mucky was there too. I whistled to them and they came running on their spindly legs. Mucky tried to snatch the fox out of my hands. There was a brief tussle, but he kept his jaw clamped tight. He was dumb, but also stubborn. In the end I gave in. The other dogs raced over to Mucky, who still had the pup's body in his mouth. Between them, they tore the pup to shreds, until he was transformed into a pile of fluff and viscera, and yet they soon grew bored. What they wanted was to hunt foxes, smell their fear. I understood them well. I was easily bored by the most horrible things. Once, I made Zaida smash her finger with the large stone we use for cracking toctes. You won't believe how easy it is to convince people to harm themselves. She crushed her finger, and yet I was bored before she was even done screaming.

I just lay there in what was left of Old Mildred's house for a long while. I didn't see Víctor return along the path, nor did I hear the voice of mamá, who'd come by looking for me, calling out my name. I didn't even sense when Mucky and the other dogs left. I could swear that a warm and gentle wind was brushing my neck, and that I was being rocked by waves. Nothing more.

It was only when mamá shook me that I awoke, and it was some time before I could understand all that she was saying. Mamá Bichito was uglier than ever, and she was scared. She had large dark circles under her eyes and hiccupped as she wept. She dragged me by the hand to the cantina where everyone had gathered, assembled like penitents, their faces red and fearful. They were pitiful to behold, so dumb and frightened. They'd been unable to track father down, and he wasn't the only person missing; several others had gone with him. I felt a powerful urge to laugh. Mamá Bichito was inconsolable, as were Carmen and Abdiel. I would have liked to have kept their faces stored inside my soul. I looked at them one by one, violently experiencing the world and all the beauty my eyes could behold, the deformities, the growths, the craters in Zaida's face, the heron-like back of Agustina, who would not stop talking, the grease dripping from Baltasar's face, the red, inflamed cheeks of Abdiel. The carnival of atrocities that is Cocuán was stranger than ever. People would have paid good money to see us: step right up and see this ghastly town.

But I was no longer frightened by it. In that moment, I no longer wished to be blind or cover my eyes; I wanted to watch them all burn, to cleanse the world and leave only the plowed hillsides in the background, that magnificent world, with no one to inhabit it. This was what I felt, what I heard. This was what I had to do: put an end to Cocuán and the rotten rat's heart that beat at its center. It was all clear, at last, as though someone had howled right in my ear, as though someone had revealed a great secret.

AGUSTINA

Those who have ears to hear, let them hear: if you listen carefully, everything speaks. Even the ripe fig as it opens says pulp, pulp, pulp! I speak because I have seen. I have come here to share a mystery, and I trust I will relate to you exactly what I saw. It happened today, during the dark hour of dawn. I awoke because my canaries were flapping around in shock, discharging watery yellowish feces, and everything smelled of chicken coop. Outside, it was different. From outside a tepid wind arrived infused with a rich scent of jasmine that spoke to me of the spring that exists at other latitudes, where the sun shines discretely. Not like here, in Cocuán, where we live so close to empty space and its dark matter that the sun is like a father, it bakes your brains or gnaws away at you, far, very far from the sheltering womb of the earth. The first thing I saw was a crippled man walking along, carefully removing his clothing. It wasn't obscene in any way. The skin of his entire body was lit up like grains of sweetcorn in the first rays of sunlight; it was more like seeing the white eyes of a dog or an old man, with that milky layer, a kind of blindness that seems to bring them close to divinity, as if we knew that, should God allow us to gaze upon him, he would look just like that: blind, his eyes covered in a pristine viscous film. I said nothing to the man. I simply looked at him. The night and the mystery were immense, and I sensed it was better to keep silent. Also, the man appeared to be in a hurry. And I would be lying if I told you I recognized him in that moment. I followed his spectral footsteps with my gaze. And he continued to walk until he was left completely naked—with a flat white backside—and then the specter-man's body went to seek shelter among the honeysuckles, winding his way through until he disappeared. Later, there were others, a pair of men and women who were already naked, moving like shadows, walking toward the craggy rocks, where the sun comes up. I didn't recognize any of them. They were a single, milk-colored mass, and I could only focus on the whiteness of their buttocks, far whiter than the rest of their skin, buttocks that had never seen the light of day, nor their own reflection in the pupils of another; that knew only the hardness of wicker and the coldness of the inert: stone, the wood of a hard bed and linoleum. Don't snigger, Esther, I prefer to say ass. Or like the French, *le cul*. You're like a grotesque set of triplets, Mercedes, Hermosina and you. You snigger like senseless teenagers, as if you can't wait to blurt out all you hold inside you: sad and sinful words. I don't give a hoot if you look at me and think "giant cowbird, giant cowbird." Among friends, you profess those fine principles. Day after day, you fulfill your obligations and then the devotion, which consists in removing pimples from your nose, or hairs from your ass. *Le cul*. You're modest to the point of tedium. But you're well aware that in the depths of your memory there is a dark night on which you hide from yourself, just like the rest of us. Is Cocuán not simply one long night? The rest of you listen to me when I tell you that one of these days you'll find the bones of some corpse hidden inside

Esther Solina's inlaid trunk, wrapped in musty black dresses, all moth-eaten, the dresses and the bones, because you're a stupid old woman and never remember to buy mothballs! That's right, that's right. Hurry away now, you'll soon get what's coming to you. In any case, let it be understood: I have only come here to tell you what I saw. I don't expect you to interpret this mystery. When have you ever done that? I considered calling out to them, to the men and women, and yet I didn't. Vitola, my parrot, was cackling loudly, but none of them turned around. And my birds continued to fly about the room, flapping clumsily, as if they'd been sleeping near poppies, drunk on white milk. As a girl, I was an enchantress of birds, did you know? When no one was looking, I would run onto the balcony and call to the tanagers. And doves came to die in my bedroom. The floor was exactly like the house I have now, a dungeon of green feces and white urine, papier-mâché composed of fecal matter. It was my scent, my mother used to say. I smelled of fruit and chaff. This was what attracted the birds. Can you smell it now? Tickling the hairs in your nose? Yuck! Yuck! Accursed old bitch! Go on. Call me that, just like Abdiel. Do you know what my mother called you, Abdiel? Sadballs! There goes that sadballs, she would say, when she saw you traipsing after Father Santamaría all day, dragging your bottle-shaped body like a punishment. And I would imagine your long, red balls, swollen like a turkey's caruncles. And even now, when you speak, I hear you gobble. Sadballs, look at me, because it's you I'm addressing now: Lucía, your wife, was with them. I recognized her by how she walks, like a deer. She was naked too, her head covered with a veil. Then I began to recognize them all, and I set off after them. I could only think that she was running from you, Abdiel, and from those excrescences, those dry sacks, like two small tumors, which you have down there. The ones that could never give her children, or perhaps it was she who never wished to bear your children, because if instead of babies she'd given birth to a couple of corncobs, you would scarcely have noticed. Did you ever once look at something until you truly saw it, Abdiel? Did you ever look at Lucía? Did you see her gnawing at her nails, nerves shriveled, wafer-thin, as if something were devouring her from the inside? Chssst. Chssst. I'll tell you what I know. It's the same to me. One time, Lucía came by my house asking me to prepare her a remedy of mugwort and rhubarb, and so I did. You all know what that's used for. I watched her arrive every morning, glancing in all directions as if someone were following her, afraid. She would enter in silence and take the concoction, saying nothing. Later, she would begin talking as if I were a priest, not looking at me. She told me so many things about her childhood, about that lousy man who was her father, about the mother who was as silent as a tree trunk, about what she remembered, because she said she remembered very little, and less and less every day. The last day she came to see me, she said, Sometimes I dream Abdiel is shrinking until he becomes a fetus, covered in liquid, like inside a mother's womb, and in that trance of being born, he begins to bawl. It isn't the crying of a baby, it's a harsh and irritating bawling, and in the next image he's fastened to my breast, feeding, and he gnaws until I bleed. That's it. She didn't even sound afraid, but rather like a dead woman, a talking corpse. Has this ever happened to you? It's an atrocity. When we women aren't dreaming of our fathers as lovers, we're dreaming of our husbands as sons. Madre mía! Madre mía! Such uproar merely for speaking the truth. All of you here know I make my living as a curandera, I hear things you wouldn't believe, and I've never wanted for food. I simply refuse to pretend I haven't done big favors for almost everyone in this cantina. Perhaps the only person who never asked me for a thing was Old Jonás, but he isn't here, he took off as well. And he wasn't drunk, but glowing, he was the first one I saw, the crippled man. Once I'd recognized him, I actually wanted him to turn around. Believe me, they were all glowing. And that frightened me. I want to tell you everything in the correct order. Make for the end in one straight line, like a girl balancing on the edge of a sidewalk—but oh! I was always the girl with grass stains on her knees. And none of you believe a word I'm saying because I live with my birds. Know that any one of my parrots or canaries, my toucans, my curiquingues or tanagers speaks more truth than a single one of you ever has. The difference is that you don't even suspect that you've been trained to parrot the same thing over and over again: conceived without sin, conceived without sin. It's fair and necessary, fair and necessary. And, nevertheless, you believe every word from men like Baltasar. If Baltasar told you, in that walrus voice of his, to sacrifice all your cattle, to slay your donkeys, your sheep, to slaughter your chickens, you'd do so without a peep. Well, you should know that I've seen him walking in the forest with girls so young it's terrifying. I didn't come here to air his secrets. But while you all ignore me, I observe you. I sit in my rocking chair to smoke and watch you, like a girl who looks at insects through a magnifying glass, until they eventually become gigantic and devour her. What's more, this is a town of lousy men. Abdiel is one, Jonás too. Baltasar is a lousy sad man. It's better that the children learn this now. Here, girls like you, Carmen, like Zaida, must surely be little women already, rolling around in secret with who knows which old man with a sickly cough who's pursuing you. If the answer is Cocuán, then what the devil is the question? The last time an outsider arrived here, it was Capa; Santamaría and Manzi don't count, they only brought more silence. Many of us were children at the time, covered in scratches and adhesive bandages, climbing fig trees and tossing avocados and toctes into large jute sacks. We never suspected we might be nurturing new monsters inside us. It was the time of the dust. The main road forced anyone travelling south to pass through here. Those beautiful years of the dust, when anything seemed possible. But the bypass cut us off and now people drive by in trucks without even catching a whiff of the fact that other men and women who were spat up by the earth are living here. We're an old and vanished town. You must realize. Nothing in Cocuán is what it seems. We're all composed of dust and evil, like nightmares. Our cemetery is a swamp sown with rotten crosses that disappear now every time the river swells. Not even our dead want to remain with us.

Shhhhh.

Listen.

I came too close to them and a hand shoved me to the ground. When that happened, I could think of nothing. I began to breathe more deeply. A terrifying sound filled my head. And, to begin with, I believed it was the wind, and yet the sound was coming from them. It was a strange melody, as if all that could be heard from the world was the crying of newborn babies or the screeching of cats in heat. Drawn out yowls. I'm not sure why that sound made me feel my breast was swollen, my heart open and enlarged; as though I had witnessed a revelation: the death of a saint or the transformation of a woman into a bird. And, though you won't believe it, all this prompted me to meditate. That sound made me kneel down. I wanted to think, wanted to understand what I was witnessing, but it was as if they were instructing me to look up at the sky and comprehend that all the stars that shone so brightly were already dead. I was thinking about all this when, from so much pounding on my head, I began to fall asleep, I was forced to slap myself to stay awake. And I crawled through the cornfields, where they had left their clothes, which now resembled dark scarecrows, dummies made of wheat spikes and sweaty rags, dead skin and brambles. That's how I found that shirt smelling of alcohol and kerosene belonging to Old Jonás, and the rectangular strip of old wool Berta's mother made her wear, and also Tadeo's shoes, chewed at the toe, but polished. Such depravity, I thought. What abandonment was revealed by their garments. Clothed or naked, they would be just as alone. I got to my feet and again ran after them, already approaching the eucalyptus forest. There wasn't a single child among them. It was then that I spotted Old Gioconda, hunched like a desiccated condor, and Berta Sotelo, at peace for once, lacking that sad expression of a miserable drunk she always wore; it was different now, the skin of her face glowed like that of a pregnant woman.

Whenever I think of the Lord, the first thing that comes to mind is the porcelain chamber pot where I used to pee as a girl, adorned with a bunch of chubby angels with wings sprouting from their butts, like bats with cherub faces. When I had to pray, I would sit before the chamber pot, look at them, and ask that they carry my prayer up to God.

God, grant me a bicolor pencil; God, grant me a mother who isn't mad; God, grant me a gigantic brother I can play with like a little boy—and the bat cherubs would stare back at me as if saying "haw haw haw." When I saw our brothers and sisters, I thought of that same chamber pot.

In that moment I wished to say to God, Lord, let me be one of them. "Haw haw haw," I heard. And do you know what I did? I ran as fast as I could, just like when I was small and would chase after tanagers in the high forest, as quick along the ground as the birds were in the sky. I ran with my arms open and came close, so close that I launched myself and grabbed one by the ankle. And when she turned around, she looked at me as if she'd seen a demon. It was Lucía, Abdiel, it was her, with her deer's legs. I thought she would offer me her hand, take me with her, but she shook her ankle as hard as she could. She denied me like a monster. And I felt an urge to kill her. I took a stone in my hand and, as I was about to release it, I thought that this could be the reason they hadn't taken me with them.

Because I was dark inside. As we all are. We hold the night inside us, because Cocuán is only night. I kept moving. I wept as I watched them disappear into the forest, full of light. I couldn't stop panting like the old woman I am, and I was dazed by the howl they emitted before the wind carried it away, far from me. Then I tripped. I fell over again. Accursed old bitch! as Abdiel says. Slumped on the ground, helpless. It was then that I began to fear for all of us, a pack of filthy, toothless wolves. The lamb in its meekness faces its killer head on, but we would rather lick his feet than see ourselves disemboweled.

That is the mystery.

Now, bite your tongues.

MANZI

I emerged from the monastery wrapped in blankets. In the darkness, they were all one being. Old Abdiel, who resembled a dodo, was at the front and talking non-stop, like a boy who lies about seeing wolves. They didn't allow me time to understand what was happening. Come, Father, come, said those voices seemingly wrenched from their tiredness. I followed them, immediately, to the main square, where they had lit a fire, as they sometimes do on very cold nights, with the most experienced leaping over the flames. But not on that night; that burning bush gave off a black wind and scorched the skin. With eyes reddened by ash, they announced we would be leaving before dawn. Men and women went to prepare for the journey.

The children formed a ring around the fire and knelt down to pray. Carmen, the lankiest and most insipid of them, rose and began separating the ashes around the bonfire. She did this with a wooden stick, before forming small mounds with her hands. Carmen's arms were plump and reached down below her knees; she resembled a scarecrow, stuffed with down, her hair in jet-black braids. The others began to recite the Lord's Prayer like a hand clapping rhyme. Our–father–who–art–in–heaven. They prayed in raised voices.

Once they had finished, Carmen—the tall one—paused. Víctor, a boy with thick hair, a bruised face and an imploring gaze, pushed himself up off the ground with his hands, wiped the dirt from his palms on his jeans and moved toward Carmen until their noses touched. She drew an ashy cross on his brow and kissed it. One by one, the rest went over and the scene was repeated. God bless us, they said in unison each time, God protect us. Only one of them, Ezequiel, when very close to Carmen, hurled a fistful of dirt that left her spluttering. No one said a thing, nor did they look at him; they were afraid of him.

I was observing them, sat under a street lamp, on the sidewalk, when Ezequiel came over with that killer's face of his and sat down next to me. To begin with, he was very quiet, then he began swatting flies with claps of his hands, before looking at his palms so he could count them. Father, he said, does God want us to obey him? Does God want me to be a magnificent boy? I wasn't sure how to answer him, and he carried on looking at me as if he believed in me, just as the ancients of these towns believed in myths. This is how they look at me sometimes, and when they do I feel afraid. In faith, there is also hatred.

In Cocuán, you will just as soon find people kneeling before a saint as sacrificing chickens outside the church doors. When I arrived in this parish, Father Santamaría, already senile and unwell, told me, Use the savagery of these people to your advantage, Manzi. They are capable of seeing miracles where none exist. They are the class of believer we spend our whole lives searching for.

A few days later, he hanged himself from one of the rafters in the monastery, in the room containing the body of that woman.

And that is what I have done. I have allowed the children to come to me. I have forbidden nothing to these people, not their customs, nor their rituals. I take advantage of their rapture to speak to them of the Lord, our God, and it is as if they were beholding him. Some say he has a great big beard, others claim he has white eyes. Though they affect to be simpletons, they walk the path between sainthood and a perverse imagination.

When the children had finished, they sat down on the sidewalk to wait for the start of the expedition. That is what they called it.

The women were already arriving from their homes, walking on bowed legs, in a hurry. They carried toquilla straw baskets, from which they took provisions, some wrapped in palm leaves, others in grubby handkerchiefs. They also carried large steaming thermoses. Esther, Mercedes and Hermosina carried nothing, their stout bodies planted beside the donkey, three housewives donning their shawls like hoods and crossing themselves ad infinitum.

The children would not stop calling to the dogs, those stinking dogs that always roamed the forest, plunging into the wilderness and returning with ticks that soon spread to the rest of us. But the dogs did not come out from wherever they were hiding. They barked and howled, sounding terrified, as the night grew.

It was Baltasar, Germán and Abdiel who lost patience and fanned out through town to look for them. They were dogs belonging to no one, filthy and matted, some with mange or muzzles covered in pimples; they refused to look you in the eye, and wouldn't enter any home unless it was to piss on the carpets. But ever since I arrived, I had always seen them hanging around the people of Cocuán. They obeyed and came running the moment anyone whistled, and then people would toss them some leftovers, some pork rinds, and the dogs went off happy. They never did any harm.

We started hearing howls and snarls that grew increasingly nasty. Baltasar came back hopping on one leg, wounded. Fucking dogs, he said. And a short while later Abdiel and Germán also returned, without the dogs, but dazed and panting. They ordered us to leave as soon as possible—in the middle of the night.

Wait a little, I said.

Quiet, Father, there's no time.

They stomped off, kicking up dust, and everyone followed. They ruled over the town.

I choked down my fear and prepared to guide them. I had walked those forests before, particularly as a new arrival, when I would lose myself there, asking God, What am I doing in this place? Why have you sent me? Who are you? And I heard nothing but a ring of silence.

The sons and daughters of Cocuán were my own personal flock. It was my duty to accompany them. We were going in search of those who were missing. At first, it all sounded absurd to me; that whole story about men and women who wandered naked toward the crag seemed like another product of these people's wild imagination, but later I thought it might be the answer I'd been waiting for, that it was my destiny to lead the town in search of their brothers and sisters; maybe then my Lord, my God, would grant me consolation.

In single file, we advanced through the shadows.

We were traveling very light. Just one donkey that carried the wrapped provisions on its back: jars of pork fat, quesillo cheese, rye bread and bottles of agua de pítimas made by the nuns, woolen blankets and cowhide rugs for camping out, if necessary. The journey was not meant to take longer than one or two days. We were only going to the crag. No one ever ventured further, for beyond it was the jungle, where beasts and men could devour you.

Agustina had seen them that very morning, heading toward the crag, where the sun came up. She was sure of that, they had gone past her house and disappeared into the forest. There was no other path to take.

Occasionally, Agustina would come up to the front and walk beside me, always to make some trivial remark. I'm sorry, Father, but you should look down at your feet from time to time. In the forest, it's good to look where you're stepping. This is what she said to me, and at that very moment I stumbled into a shallow ditch, and she just stood there, with her rags and a barely perceptible smile.

I wanted to forget about this incident, and so continued walking, my flock behind me. We moved away from town, entered the forest, and did not look back; if we had, we might perhaps have seen a light someone had left burning, a last sign of our departure, like the tables left set when war arrives.

In the distance, a cock crowed.

I have never revealed this to anyone, but with my flock I felt like a pregnant fish, swollen, full of eyes inside me; my gaze was their gaze, but they saw things I could not. They witnessed the depths of the sea and yet were unable to tell me about them. Mothers must feel the same way with their babies, must want to be them, be inside a uterus, a warm and absolute universe that only they can know, the sole record of the world's secret: the womb, the reflection of the cosmos, the source.

Once more, as we crossed the pastureland, where bony old cows roamed, Agustina approached and began unleashing a stream of nonsense. How she thought that Nebuchadnezzar might have been happier with eagles' feathers and the long claws of a bird. How she couldn't understand why that man had repented in the middle of his transformation. It was as if he'd finally opened his eyes, she said. "The depths of the sea," I thought. The Bible seemed to her like a series of vulgar mishaps, metamorphoses that never reached completion, as if the world were the property of some fraudulent magician. She was so lost, poor thing. And I was afforded no time to respond, because it was then that I stumbled over a lump, a dead barn owl. I bent down to pick it up. It was still warm, its eyes open.

A bird is a warning, Father, said Agustina; the bird is also the pauper's only sacrifice.

Then I sensed her spectral breath, composed of chicha and chewed tobacco.

My flock, my fish, my eyes, so far from me.

It was almost daybreak when we reached the pine forest. We came to a halt. The women lay down the rugs and served agua de pítimas and bread with pork fat to everyone, while the children snaked their way between the dark trunks. When dawn arrived, a swollen red sun appeared to penetrate the trunks and stain them. The children had already started dipping into that pool of scarlet. The men and women continued to eat, biting into their bread with agua de frescos, that cold herbal tea which left white spittle at the corners of their mouths, while the world turned from red to gray, from gray to white, in a dawn like that inside a shoebox, like every dawn in Cocuán, that town with its harsh climate.

Baltasar, Germán and Abdiel stood up and began moving away. We're off to make water, they said, we're going for a piss. I joined them, and we walked a while in silence as the morning brightened. Baltasar began telling us how, when he was small, that forest didn't exist. He himself had helped to plant it. A bunch of bald and scrawny monks gave us the small, pyramidal saplings, he said, full of sharp branches, and made us plant them at dead of night, at new moon, and the ancient forest was buried, like a corpse.

I thought of those Franciscan brothers, living in a town like that, their cassocks getting covered in mud; despising those people, seeing in them and the forest nothing but wickedness.

The pines appeared to devour everything and vomit only dry leaves, splinters and twigs that prickled when you walked over them. Our forest is buried under this one, said Baltasar. His voice began to peter out, leaving me with an image of the exodus of hundreds of birds, tree trunks like interred bones. He had already selected a tree on which to urinate, and the rest of us went to choose others, further away.

Abdiel asked Baltasar if Berta Sotelo had given him any money before she went missing. Baltasar said Berta always wanted money for drink, but that, luckily, she had paid off all her interest the month before. If I had not been aware of these people's vices, I would not have understood a thing. Baltasar also said that all the missing owed him money, and this was why he was going after them. He said he knew things he could use against them, that Tadeo was thinking of going to work on a banana plantation, very far away, that Jonás had squandered his father-in-law's inheritance. Germán chuckled and Abdiel stayed silent. I realized this was because his wife was among the missing, and now he knew she had debts of her own.

It has nothing to do with money. I understood this long ago. All in Cocuán take part. Loan and collect. They call it chulco. They loan money and fight over money. The bills that circulate in town are so worn you can almost see through them. It's like a game: under the table they're all placing bets, they take your hand, and if you refuse to pay, they break it, if you refuse to pay, they crush it, if you refuse to pay, they lop it off. Games have rules and consequences. This is what attracts them. It has nothing to do with money.

I made no effort to deter this. The stories of loans, of interest and collections, occupied the evenings of the town. I did not punish them or mention the sin of usury in my sermons. For a long time, I tried to watch and listen to how these things played out in town, and I could draw only two conclusions. One: in Cocuán, chulco is a kind of birthright; two: it stops them killing each other. Because a corpse can't pay, one of them once told me, Know this, Father, a corpse can't pay.

Returning to the camp they had pitched, I found the donkey packed and ready. We resumed our journey. Rows of pine trees like needles. Over time, the forest had spread; it now covered more than a hectare. We planned to reach the high forest before midday. We walked steadily. Up there, the animals scarcely showed signs of life; as we walked, we spooked the occasional lizard, or some child startled the occasional sparrow with their slingshot. For them, this was all an adventure. They were happy and content.

Suddenly, a shouting match flared up. When I turned to look, the women had formed a ring around Filatelio and Baltasar. Filatelio was the town fool. The man would eat anywhere and slept in the monastery. Sometimes, at night, I would find him kissing the lifeless hands of Mildred and beat him. Then he would go off into a corner and howl. I didn't know why Santamaría had never gotten rid of that body. I couldn't do it either, but I never let anyone in town see it—they would have lost their minds. Filatelio could be tasked with any kind of manual labor, and sometimes he touched the hands of women; he was able to tell if they were pregnant, if it was a boy or a girl. Filatelio knew things. I did not allow him to touch me. At that moment, one of them was on top of the other: Baltasar was pressing down on Filatelio's throat with his forearm and had his other hand raised, holding a large, sharp stone. I ran over to stop them. By the time I arrived, Abdiel and Germán already had them separated, and Filatelio was screaming, Living flesh is wicked, living flesh is very wicked! I felt as if the day had suddenly gone dark. My eyes went cloudy. "Turn on the light," I thought. I don't know why. I felt lightheaded and confused.

In the forest there is no light, said Agustina.

When I turned to look at her, she simply added, I know everything, Father. In the forest there is no light, only the sun that shines.

In the distance, the crowing of a cock could be heard.

Why did you say that to him, my child? I asked Filatelio.

But he was looking up at the sky, chewing empty-mouthed, and said nothing.

Esther asked, What did he say? What did he say?

Living flesh is very wicked, I replied.

Who said that? asked Baltasar. That one tripped me over, but he never said a word.

I responded that Filatelio had said it, he said living flesh is wicked.

They both stared back at me. My flock, my believers. All eyes watched me from within, wide eyes staring inside my tummy.

I was frightened and proposed we all sit down to pray for a moment. They began taking their seats, as I had instructed, one by one, in single file. I led the prayer. Our Father, I began, but instead of praying, the townsfolk intoned a song that went:

> The straw I set alight in the mountains
> Must still be burning,
> Must still be blazing.
> If it still burns,
> If it still blazes,
> Douse it with your tears ...

Against all my expectations, I did not want the singing to stop. How to start at the beginning? Since arriving in Cocuán, I had tried to eliminate everything separating me from my parishioners. Was I always like this? Who can say. I'm not sure of anything. I simply wanted to keep them close. Is that so terrible? I let my hands go slack and joined in with their song.

We set off again. The children were running all around me, picking up pine nuts and flinging them over their heads. Víctor was the only one permitted to carry a machetillo, and he was tasked with marking the trees in case we got lost. The old women were all hunched over, except Agustina, who always walked with her chin up. The pine forest was becoming interspersed with small bushes, pear trees, apple trees, great goldenberry shrubs and nasty little ponds that reeked of stagnant water.

I asked to stop for a breather. I couldn't carry on. I was still dizzy and decided to sit while the women went off to the ponds to pee, lifting their skirts and squatting down like brooding hens. I closed my eyes for a few minutes, because my eyelids and temples were throbbing. Then I saw Mildred's body, that body which shone in the dark depths of the monastery, a dead body full of light and warmth—impossible.

Why do you make me suffer, Lord?

Then I heard it again, now all of them were repeating it, Living flesh is wicked. Living flesh is very, very wicked.

Enough! I yelled.

And when I opened my eyes, they were all around me with those sunken cheeks and mistrustful eyes, staring at me like I was a madman. The children had gone on ahead, and were skipping blithely.

The hatred arrived.

How to start at the beginning? As a boy, I used to pee in the hollows of tree trunks and the forest was inside me.

Tell me, Lord, why did you send me?

A ring of silence around me. A Stygian forest.

Come, Father, come, they encouraged me, pityingly.

With the help of Agustina, I proceeded along the remainder of the path. How I detested her. The ground of dry leaves began to give way to small marshes and clumps of tussock grass that appeared to have sprung up at that moment, bursting from the ground.

"This is not such a big deal," I thought.

Altitude sickness, I said, I think I've come down with soroche.

And I took Agustina's shoulder, which smelled of dead barn owl, and leaned against it.

The pine trees began to thin out. The sky cleared and it was blue. A very fine film of mist settled on the bushes, the rocks and all of us. We were like statues covered in dust. We had finally reached the high forest, the original forest.

It was after midday and the sun was beating down on my head. The sky filled with tanagers, flying in a disordered group. Agustina ran with open arms, looking up at them and yelling god bird, god bird and other nonsense. The increased humidity caused my breathing to become labored, agitated; I could feel the water making space inside my lungs, filling them with tiny droplets, internal perspiration. I was forced to take a seat, and suddenly I felt a kind of uncertain peace, suffused with something spectral. The single file dissolved, my flock scattered, moving happily among the forest and its wonders.

The children vanished quickly. One minute, I would see them catching frogs, the next, searching for duck eggs in the totora reeds. The women pulled up herbs and slipped them between their bosoms. When they returned, they smelled of geraniums and passion flowers. And the men ran toward Uza's fall to refresh themselves and skip stones. Everything was finally peaceful and seemed to be following the proper order.

Then Filatelio sat down beside me. He seemed to be chewing, but his mouth was empty, and I could feel his breath very close to my ear.

His breath was cold and damp, like the forest itself.

Living flesh is very wicked, he whispered to me, and then he howled.

I wet myself.

My thighs were warm.

Now what? I thought.

There was no path to lead me back, nor plans to return home. There was no home. This was my life, these were my parishioners, Cocuán my place; the town, my personal flock. They were a pack of savages and I was filled with dark forebodings. I should lead them to the heart of the forest. Like when I was a boy and would linger there to witness God. I peed in tree hollows. Days went by and I grew hungry. I survived on roots. I never saw him. When I returned, I told people I had seen him and everyone believed me because I was not a boy who lied about seeing wolves. They believed me mercilessly.

I took Filatelio's face in my hands. I looked into his eyes, which were large and moving quickly. They were not the eyes of a halfwit or a fool. They were those of a wolf. The others were all far away, there was no one to hear what I had to tell him. I leaned in toward his mouth, breathing in his warm breath.

I never saw God, I confessed, but I have seen the body.

Filatelio howled.

The heart of the forest was inside me. He carried a machetillo in his belt; I seized it and, before the others could return, I did it. The sharp blade sliced through my ear. There was no pain, only the fading echo of that howl. Filatelio licked the warm blood. I did the same thing with the other ear and saw the world turn gray and dark. It was nighttime and no one would switch on the light. Something strange must have been happening, because I could still hear the words, Living flesh is wicked. Living flesh is very wicked.

In the distance, a cock crowed.

CARMEN

You didn't know a thing about the town. What for? You said this was not a town, but the agony of the countryside. You said you didn't want to grow old in an old place.

If I'd had any pride, Tadeo, I would have stayed down there, in Cocuán. In that agony. Instead, I was walking with a handful of rheumatic old people and a priest with no ears. His head had been bandaged up by Abdiel with some old woolen socks on which the blood traced lilies and zinnias.

Manzi traveled like that, bandaged, on the back of the donkey. He would look down at his empty hands from time to time and then slap his left palm hard, like a mother with a disobedient child: "bad boy, bad, bad." He was the mother; he was the child.

Alongside him walked the eldest, hunched over, telling each other things and quickly forgetting them. Every once in a while, you would hear, What did you say? What was it she said? Mercedes travelled with Chabuca, her red face pressed against her mother's back, in silky sleep. It was hard for Mercedes to walk with the girl on her back, but neither she, nor Hermosina, nor Esther seemed troubled. Who knows, perhaps their stout bodies were filled with feathers, because they advanced lightly, though panting, and would not stop whispering litanies. Agustina ran, skipped, picked up flat stones and slipped them inside her left pocket after sucking on them, and sometimes she also sang. Víctor was limping, but he carried the food supplies with Ezequiel. Zaida, María and I went last, sad and gloomy. María wasn't looking at us, she was in another world. Zaida clasped my hand as if she were afraid. Occasionally, Esther would turn around and ask her if she'd cleaned herself thoroughly before we left, if she'd hung the washing, if she'd prayed. At least we would have been able to laugh at them all, Tadeo, as we always did, laugh at Hermosina and her rubbery ankles, and how she clung to Baltasar for the entire journey, at Mercedes, at Esther with her face like a tight ass, at Abdiel, at my father, Germán, who stumbled over everything, like a drunk, laugh at Cocuán and our own bad luck for having been born there. But I was as alone as a specter, a mallow plant.

We circled the lake and could hear only the deer, calling to each other somewhere in the distance. A forest is a black hole, what it traps is never released, not even light can escape it. A forest is the stillness of God, the place where flowers climb and fall, a wind containing many winds, a snare in which the dead find themselves strung up like hares, wailing and screeching. But you did not love our forest, you seemed sad and old, like the rest of us.

Even as a young girl, I already knew how to distinguish between the bleats of a deer, do you remember? A long bleat wasn't the same as a short one, I would tell you, a series of short bleats was a call for you to follow them, to look for them. By that point, Tadeo, you had already set yourself before me and, taking my hand, told me I had a very pretty name. And I taught you how to dance, and we planted hummingbird eggs thinking birds were born from the earth, elegantly shaking their wings off, and we dipped our dirty feet in the same washbasin and prayed together to Our Lady of La Leche until the day we touched her nipple and could have sworn the hard paint was warm, but nobody believed us. We were strangers to fatigue and the smell of underarms. Your mother always told us off for going around dirty and matted. Forgive me, tía, I would say, and she would fix me with that cockeyed stare that didn't frighten you but gave me the shivers.

We continued walking and María began to look increasingly weak; she was pale and occasionally stopped to spew up nothing but yellowish bile, because she refused to eat. Ezequiel didn't even glance at her, but Víctor wiped her mouth. I remember how you used to tell me they were very strange. You wouldn't let me go near their house or Mucky, their dog. You said they were sick with rage. Maybe you were right; Ezequiel was a little scary, he gave the impression that at any moment he might pull out a machete and butcher us all, but Víctor always seemed to me like a sickly child, and I liked to believe deep down he was already dead, and this made him inoffensive, a part of my world of the dead.

Esther made us pray the Rosary as we walked, running our thumbs over invisible beads. I prayed for you, Zaida just mumbled, and María prayed desperately for Old Jonás. And where were you all, Tadeo? Why wouldn't you come back? María carried fear in her eyes, some kind of horror that pursued us all along our journey, and which she soon embraced, without a whimper. Sometimes she would bend down to pick violets, saying, They always go and sprout beside the nettles, much like my sorrows and my blessings. As with all mothers in Cocuán, she spoke the language of litanies, of obedience, of the mercy of Christ. We, on the other hand, knew words they did not: cranny, sediment, lycopod, puzzlegrass, pistil. Our words transformed the Lamb of God into an aerolite, Tadeo, hurtling down to earth. And when we saw a shooting star, we asked it to take away the sin of the world.

Past the waterfall, the trees became covered in moss, the flowers very small, colored with joy, like candy. Bringing up the rear were Abdiel, my papá and Baltasar. They trod on the flowers without even looking at them. Whenever you saw a flower, you would cry viva, viva! And everything appeared to listen to you and grow, as in an antediluvian world of tall mushrooms, damp and shady.

But you were gone, Tadeo, and for me love had become an incantation. So I did my best to spot a hare along our way.

Nothing moved among the tussock grass, only the brooks that brought down icy water and made you want to jump in and splash; the marshes were mirages and the rushes stood very still, receiving the sunlight, and yet there was no one to look at them, it was all a trick, a hypocrisy to be here and not enjoy it. How many times had we walked across those same water mattresses and let ourselves be enraptured by the dampness and the cold, hypnotized by the scent of passion flowers, which snakes through the air and grips you, but on that day, when we went looking for them, looking for you, we were like sad monks, observing the fruit of a tree and able to think only of good and evil.

The sun was already escaping from behind the crag when, from among the mossy rocks and marshes, a hare came darting out. I immediately lost sight of it. Magic resides not in the hand that pulls the rabbit from the hat, but in the hare that moves from one world to another when it slips into its burrow in the forest, the black hole. A hare is not a hare, it is a witch. That's what they taught us, or what you and I always wanted to believe. Hares had conspired together to conjure up the world. I spat on the ground in the place I had last seen it and said, Turn Tadeo Lazlo into an old hunchback.

You would end up as a hunchback, Tadeo. The beginnings of a small hump were already noticeable on your back, like Old Gioconda. And one day I would go past and, not even looking at you, cross the street. I would be indifferent to you, nurturing my love like a wild cat.

So be it.

So be it, echoed the tall frailejones and the mushrooms looking up at me from the ground: glaucous statues and floating heads.

Father Manzi fell from the donkey. He was still staring at his empty palms. Abdiel and Víctor picked him up again and together lifted him back onto the donkey, placing his hands in his lap and covering him with a poncho. Agustina carried his ears wrapped in a bloodied handkerchief in her right pocket, and sometimes she would slip her hand inside and caress them like an amulet. I was always envious of the secrets kept by Agustina; she was the only one I never made fun of, and I never confessed to you either, Tadeo, how deep down in my heart I wished to be the daughter of that wicked woman, as they referred to her in town, because she knew things we did not, she understood the language of the wind and smelled of bird; and I wanted her to teach me to bewitch you and the birds, so none of you would leave me, and I wanted to join forces with her on those nights of tepid wind, with the birds all around us, flying and dancing, drunk on white milk.

Beyond the crag, a clearing opened out. The wind at our backs propelled us toward it. We stepped firmly, yet on the inside we were dragging our feet. The grass was fresh and soft. That forest, Tadeo, knows nothing of growing old: it becomes unhinged, climbing and falling only to return to the earth and renew itself. In the forest, everything seems so far away, but where were you? The last person to see you was her, Agustina, who would touch Manzi's ears and occasionally take out a hoop of bird beaks she shook like a tambourine, as if this were all just a children's game.

I imagined you dancing with the dead, alongside dwarves and witches around a deer, the one the ancients said we would encounter when we died, hidden in the forest, with a gaze of animal fire; a deer that is all women and all men, a deer that runs and blazes through the world without anyone seeing.

I didn't want to think you had betrayed me, Tadeo, I preferred to believe you were dead, in the same way that children die in forgotten towns, of nameless things, infested with lice, with fevers that come and go: plethoric, surrendered to the purest deliriums.

Before passing the crag, we rested. Víctor and Ezequiel set down what they were carrying on their backs, Esther and Mercedes unloaded the baskets and spread the blanket so we could all take a breather. Zaida would not have released my hand even if she'd collapsed onto the ground, she clasped it with her sweaty palm, as frightened as the smallest rabbit kits that are born last and grow no bigger than a mouse—they could live hidden in teacups, except that they tremble with cold and soon died. I sat her down beside me and heard her pulse racing. But she refused to remain seated, quickly kneeling down with her legs pressed firmly together and not meeting anybody's eye. I didn't know what she was hiding, why she was so scared, but I could imagine.

Esther started shrieking; she and María had glanced inside the baskets and sprung back like fleas. All the food was covered in worms. Father Manzi took some in his hands and stared at them with wide eyes, before opening his mouth and swallowing them down happily. Corpus Christi, he said, and burst out laughing. Abdiel bellowed, Order! order! and Baltasar undid his belt, it seemed he was going to whip us all. Bad boy, bad, bad. He lashed the earth, which was entirely blameless. All of a sudden, they both turned, and then the old women, Hermosina and Mercedes, started screaming, and I wanted to make a run for it, and Ezequiel cursed, Son of a fucking bitch! And Zaida didn't want to turn around, because she was afraid, she was always afraid. When I turned, I saw Filatelio pouring away all the water in the thermoses, howling, as he ran through the tussock grass, and that laughter infected me as well.

I was inclined to think this must be the end. Everything had been spoiled, it was time to turn around and head back to Cocuán, to begin the eternal wait for your return. But we lined up once more. Baltasar gave Filatelio a good lashing, but he just laughed and howled, and Manzi did the same. He carried on like that, tied up on top of the donkey and howling. We followed the path, with something resembling fear deep inside us, parting bejuco vines and achupallas, knowing that beyond the crag there would be no other choice. If you lay beyond there, Tadeo, we would not be able to look for you. The whole expedition would have been in vain. Hilario had once ventured past there, do you remember that story? That's how they made sure we didn't escape. Don't go beyond the forest, they told us, the earth will swallow you up like it did Hilario. We all knew Hilario was out there somewhere, changed, transformed, deranged and savage. Who knows what happened to him. Some nights we heard nothing but a howl that came from far away, bringing bugs out from under their rocks. He hadn't been swallowed by the earth, he'd been swallowed by the jungle, an even older and more devious forest.

The crag was the hardest part. Ezequiel and Víctor went first, then Zaida, me, and little Chabuca, who'd been sleeping on her mother's back for almost the entire journey and now walked bow-legged and half-dazed between the rocks and forest, which had been intermingling since the dawn of time: a love with no witnesses. We all moved in silence, panting.

Baltasar, my papá and Abdiel sat awaiting their turn; they were three great fat children. Their childhood eyes must surely have been watching them from the forest, the damp tree trunks, the oldest lichens, watching them and recalling a time when they were agile and even seemed to carry the clamor of the birds inside them, but they had killed off the homunculi that inhabited them, now buried under thick layers of dust and blubber. And they did not feel ashamed. Beside

Baltasar sat Hermosina, red and bloated, with that lethargy of a cow, a stout body and skinny legs.

Víctor and Ezequiel announced they were going on a reconnaissance expedition. We would wait for them at the highest point of the crag, sitting side-on like goats, who seem to float on mountains, ignoring gravity, believing that the vertical, the horizontal and the world all listen to them.

I couldn't understand why you'd gone off with the rest, why you hadn't simply run far away. To where there were fish, bananas, beaches, heat, slime on the rocks. And why you hadn't taken me with you.

It was always you who slept on the ground those afternoons we spent in the barn, shelling peas from their pods with our wrinkled fingers. And after our siesta, everything would smell of stalks and greenery, and this made you think of the smallness of our sky, of wanting to go far away, toward heat and humidity, because you had another world inside you.

In Cocuán, so little was known about all this that we ended up believing the world was tall and cold, like a sleepy castle in the mist, with a god who huddles up inside, and a tiny sky.

Nobody in Cocuán believed in the abundance of sky.

If loving meant believing, then in that moment I professed my faith in the dilated sky, in embalsados, those floating islands of tangled vegetation, in herons, in pampas grass, striped rosemallow, curupí trees, the maned wolf and the marsh deer. And I wanted you like never before, I wanted you dead beneath the ground, so I could become your secret widow and bring stiff carp to your graveside, the ones we used to fish out of the lake and then watch leap up and catch the sunlight, glinting for a second before returning to the water; so I could weep over you every night, Tadeo, and never think of anything else again, because the dead envelop everything. Or that's what my mother always taught me. Our dead joined us at the table in the dishes my mother continued to serve for the rest of her life, until she too died, and it was the dead who slept inside their locked bedrooms for perpetuity, while we lay flat on the floor of the house, like shadows.

Do you remember how, one day, we entered my dead brother's bedroom and felt like *we* were the ghosts? Covered in dust, clumsy, badly dressed, we ruined that immaculate room.

I wanted you dead, Tadeo, but wanting you dead was also to want the best for you.

Víctor and Ezequiel appeared atop the rocks, like giants, waving their hands in the distance as if saying "come." The sun was setting and the sky turned red for a moment, but by the time we all stood up together, our hearts toward them, it was already gray. And we kept up our pace, as though that last stretch were easy, sweating and panting. We approached. Not knowing.

Yet all of a sudden, Ezequiel fell. Víctor stood staring at him, not turning his face away. We ran toward them. When we were so close that we could almost make out the jungle that continued on the other side of the crag—the warm grass now dark because the sun was departing, the clouds in the distance gray, heralding the night—we sensed a weight. Ezequiel was lying face-down on the ground.

They didn't give us time to understand; we were blind birds, and the sky was sown with doubt. We all stopped. Only Baltasar moved forwards.

There, someone yelled.

Baltasar yelled too, but louder: There! There they are.

And he ran back over to where we were, slipping on the rocks, falling, dragging himself through the grass.

It was Víctor who saw you first. Using my hand as a visor, I tried to locate you. Behind the crag, there you were, Tadeo, observing us through the concave rocks, hidden as inside the dark womb of your mother, and I wept because I could feel you watching us with a troubled expression, full of horror. You feared us. We all froze before this vision, except Baltasar, rubbing his grazed knees. From on high, Víctor called to us.

And I looked at you as though for the first time. As though I were a newborn. And the others—the ones who had left—were all with you. Small, due to the distance, huddled together, fearful, hunkered down. The bald heads, the naked bodies, everything Agustina had described. And, as one, you howled.

VÍCTOR

Tangled clouds set in and the earth swelled. Then you saw the wind sever three branches from the quishuar tree. It was a wind of angry saints that came from the east and which the forest received reluctantly. You picked up the stone with a spinning wheel–shaped stain made from your brother's blood and hurled it far away. And you pounded on your temples with your fists.

You carried Ezequiel in your arms. He had his eyes closed. He no longer made you feel afraid. That isn't true. He frightened you more than ever, because he was dark like in your mother's womb, where he'd already started threatening you even before opening his eyes, looming over you while, huddled, you buried your chin between your knees and brought your elbows in together, trying not to touch his cold skin. You would have let yourself be killed in order to remain there, inside your mother's tummy, where it was so good, so mindless, so crazed.

With your brother in your arms, you looked up at the sky: total darkness. Then you saw the Serpent and the Llama, and the two constellations foretold of blood on the leaves. Your brother moaned and you bent down to lay him on the grass, at the foot of the quishuar, asking that this sacred tree swallow him; but the quishuar didn't swallow children, it spat them up from the depths of the earth like those plump fig-leaf gourds spat up by the vegetable gardens of Cocuán. You wanted to leave your brother there. But there were witnesses. You considered that perhaps no one is truly good, because there are always witnesses. The thought made your heels go cold and you shook your feet to scare off all that night.

First you spotted Carmen, and she wasn't alone, she was approaching with Zaida and Filatelio, who each gripped her by a hand, him walking with his arms dangling like a lunatic, and behind them came the donkey with Father Manzi on top, and Baltasar, who was limping and cursing, and behind him all the rest. They tiptoed over the rocks and forest. You beckoned to them, but it seemed they couldn't see you, they just kept walking on tiptoe, climbing up the crag and coming toward you. When they walked like that, they revealed those dove's breasts possessed by all in Cocuán, like red brocket deer rearing up on hind legs. The scene was ridiculous. On the right, those who'd stayed behind, a band of orphans who trudged through the forest like castigated children. On the left, those who'd launched the stone that injured your brother, the naked ones, the other side of this world, those who'd left invoking chaos, attacking you with stones or simply defending themselves, who can say, but by that point all of them had vanished.

You took off your shoes and walked toward your people, your group. Although you no longer knew who your people were. If you'd had to choose between the living and the dead, things would have been easier. One should always side with the dead, because the dead don't go around worrying their brains out.

Not so loud, Esther, they'll hear, said Baltasar.

They've gone, responded Germán.

Who can be sure they aren't still out there hiding,

the savages, with an outstretched hand and a strong arm, said Hermosina.

They put me in mind of my mother, said Baltasar, that bitch used to throw stones when she flew off the handle.

Wash your mouth out, snapped Esther.

It's a beautiful night and the sun is shining, said Agustina.

My God, be quiet, said Hermosina.

Living flesh alive is, wicked is, wicked does, whispered Manzi, and then he took his head in his hands and howled. Abdiel gave him a smack across the chops.

We must go see them, said Carmen, they're sure to still be there, behind the rocks.

There's no reason to hurry, said Baltasar.

They were all so naked, as if they knew no sin. Madre mía! said Esther.

We need to convince them to come back, said Baltasar, they all owe me money, all of them.

What can they be thinking? asked your mother.

A while ago, your husband said something that made me wonder, said Germán.

That's right, Old Jonás told us how his father used to say that in this town we needed to stop making bricks and go look for the veins, said Abdiel.

A mine? asked Baltasar.

Copper, silver, even gold. More still if you head out toward the jungle, responded Germán.

We can't all go. We don't know what they want, said Esther, crossing herself.

They conversed while crouching down, then formed a circle around your brother, and María, your mother, raised his head and lay it in her lap, while the rest gazed upon him like a martyr. He'd woken up now and was feeling his head, gingerly, his fingers stained with blood. He was sprawled out, face lying on top of your mother, body in the grass.

Esther and Mercedes unloaded the baskets from the donkey, which was lying down, its front and hind legs folded in. You felt an urge to lie down next to it and sleep, leave them to deal with things, let them bring the others back, and the next day you could all return to Cocuán together, to the town you'd left only the night before and which now seemed as distant as those towns to the south, as the jungle, where they say God does not reside. You wondered how to know for certain whether God resided in Cocuán or the crag, or further beyond that. Where the threshold lay that divided God's territories from the rest, and what it would look like. You considered something even more extraordinary: if Cocuán was a town of God, then perhaps the territories where he did not reside were a celebration.

I'll go find them myself and bring them back to you, you said.

Everyone roared with laughter and the clamor of the birds rose up behind them. You crouched down to gather some lumps of panela sugar and what little was left of the rye bread that had been rescued from the worms, but you did not eat any of it, instead stowing it in your pocket without knowing why. You were also unsure why you'd offered to go. The laughter continued, and then you saw your mother, who held her hand out to you with the gaze of a deer, as though asking your forgiveness, sorry for what she'd said when the stone struck your brother: Not my Ezequiel!

Quit your laughing. Maybe it's not such a bad idea, said Baltasar, go tell your father that whatever it is they're planning, we'll help, but they should come back first.

When they see you coming, show them your hands, said Esther, so they aren't frightened of you.

Larks ask the heavens to rid them of such blindness. They aren't coming back. They're in the trance of being born, said Agustina, we might as well head back.

Shit-eater, said Germán, approaching her with his palm raised.

Agustina took the parish priest's ears from her pockets and brought them up near her own. Then she howled. Manzi howled too, and even when Abdiel smacked him across the chops, he didn't stop.

Lord, deliver us from this one, said Esther. Did no one teach you to be God-fearing, you wicked woman.

Filatelio howled too, even more loudly than the others. Everyone looked at them, fearfully. The fear deformed their features. But you weren't scared, you would have joined in with the howling if you'd known the correct way to do it, like they did, like animals. Carmen and Zaida started crying and Baltasar went and grabbed Agustina from behind, covering her mouth and telling her that if she carried on that way, she'd pay for it. When he released her, she simply stared at everyone and said, May the heavens and the earth curse you! She took Filatelio by the hand, and they went to sit on the other side of the quishuar, which was large enough to play veinticino y un quemado. Manzi stood up and followed them, the donkey trailing behind, its grizzled jaws searching for some bale of hay on which to gorge itself. There they remained, seated.

Baltasar and Germán bared their teeth, as though smiling, but in reality they were plotting torture. They were not men who could put up with screaming, or crying, or laughter. One time, you had helped Baltasar to plow his land. In thanks, he'd given you oatmeal with mutton to eat, then told you to feed it to his mother, even showing you how to do it. He held out a spoon to the old woman and, on opening her mouth, his mother had moaned, you assumed in pain; then Baltasar raised his hand to the woman, who instantly recoiled, in fear, before opening her mouth just wide enough to swallow down the pap, pinching the back of her hand all the while.

I'll go, you said again.

And your brother raised his eyes to look at you and right then you could have burst into tears, because he spoke to you from the very center of his body, where they'd burned the umbilical cord and bonded you together with fire, words and skin. And it was all your fault for going to look for your father: what person wanted a father like that, a wound, someone who would surely build a new world using the very stone with which he'd killed you. Then you approached Him, Ezequiel, and since you were incapable of hurting him, you knelt down beside him, because you had done so from your time in the womb, always prostrating yourself before Him, the one you imagined as a centaur: a god, a tyrant.

A great wind swept in, this time seemingly coming from the ground, and the women took out the woolen blankets. Mercedes and Esther swaddled Chabuca and Zaida and lay down beside them, while the others continued to eat the remaining crumbs of food.

Abdiel will go with you, said Baltasar.

Abdiel leapt up like a thieving monkey and launched a gob of spit at Baltasar that flew into his eyes. Baltasar didn't hesitate to retaliate with a stomp. But it was he himself who suddenly let out another howl and began moaning that his feet burned like fire.

It'll be gout, said Esther.

Then, along with Mercedes and Hermosina, he knelt down to pray: an Our Father, an Ave Maria, and Deliver us, Lord, from Evil.

You'll go with him because your wife is over there, or doesn't that matter to you? said Baltasar, springing to his feet.

Fucking moron, said Abdiel, bending down to search among the rags for some tobacco.

Take the oil lamp, said Esther.

If we don't return by sunrise, head on back to town, said Abdiel.

We'll cross that bridge when we come to it, said Baltasar.

Carmen was still crying, and she grabbed you by the hem of your pants and begged you to take her with you.

Well, you must be a whore then, said Germán, her father, sitting her down on the ground beside Zaida and Chabuca, who were busy pulling up grass and flowers.

There was no water left thanks to Filatelio, so while instructing you to go with Abdiel, they sent Germán to the lake to fill the thermoses, and you saw Baltasar gathering twigs and branches for a campfire. By the time you left with Abdiel, you carried smoke in your eyes, for they'd already lit the fire.

Abdiel advanced silently with the oil lamp in hand. The flame was already flickering out. He kept his body very rigid, as if he were about to fold in half; from time to time he would stop, crack his neck and stretch his fingers. You weren't sure what to say to each other, you couldn't recall ever having talked to him before. You held out your hand with a few lumps of panela sugar, which he refused and then continued panting, not really sure which way to go. You moved like the wind, tearing out the branches of shrubs, the cold in your bare feet, which no one had noticed.

Yet that cold caused a tingling sensation all over your body, you stepped on lichens and trickling water and wanted to go quickly, as if possessed, but Abdiel, that old fat-cheeks, was exasperatingly slow. The further you went, the more the forest filled up with large mossy rocks. There was no horizon. Only a cold dark area of stony ground you slowly entered like the womb of a fossil. A fine mist streamed between the rocks and Abdiel said you should take a break, that you weren't going to find them in all that darkness, and you told him to wait there, that you'd go on ahead.

Lean up against that rock. I'll come back and find you. I want to pray first, you said.

You lied, you didn't want to pray, you wanted to get away from the old man and strike out on your own. Abdiel heeded your words and leaned back, holding the oil lamp out to you and taking a little tobacco from his patched pocket, standing there chewing with his loose gums.

You followed the only path through the chuquiraguas and tussock grass snaking between the rocks. You extinguished the flame in case you should need it later and allowed your eyes to grow accustomed to that darkness. You rubbed them hard as you walked, taking pleasure in it, and the darkness you had inside became greater than the darkness outside. Suddenly, you heard the thud of hooves against the earth. At first you imagined the donkey had followed you, but then, from behind one of those rocks as high as walls, you saw a white forehead appear, and a pair of nostrils—so large you could have stuck your whole fist inside—opening and closing. When it revealed itself fully, the horse had a long black tail, and when you moved closer, you patted its neck and saw those black eyes amidst a white coat that seemed to light up the forest. From where you stood, you could already make out the jungle, and that apparition caused a throbbing in your temples and your sex, though you did not know why.

You focused on the horse. You'd never been so close to one; it seemed to you that, in comparison to that horse, any man was filled with wicked intentions. You attempted to mount it, but you're clumsy and you landed on your backside, bare feet in the air and covered in wet grass, which the horse licked happily. You remembered you were carrying panela sugar and held your hand out with a few pieces, which the horse immediately gobbled up with its loose teeth, looking at you with those black eyes, and you didn't know why you felt a sudden desire to howl, dance and sing. And as soon as you did this, you also felt feverish and wished to get undressed, and only then, with your skin cold and full of night, were you able to mount it, propping your hand against the crumbly surface of the rock.

The horse burst into a gallop and you felt the cold wind that moved through your pores and told you things you couldn't understand but knew to be true, and you didn't stop, not you or the horse, crossing that labyrinth of stone as though racing toward the devil, laughing all the way.

This is how you traversed lost paths, the rocks standing before you like tombstones, and yet the horse seemed to know where it was going, as if it had some shortcut inscribed in the memory of its hooves, a map hidden in the soft area between heel and toe. You would have liked to look at it. One time, your mother had told you that nothing was as calming as looking at maps, touching their texture of worn, dried skin, but you had never seen a map, nor had you touched skin like that, because your father wouldn't let you, it gave him the creeps, and he would chase you away with slaps.

You rode for a long time between rocks that turned everything dark; it appeared you were going around in circles, as if the rocks marked out a walled labyrinth that made the stars shine brighter: the Serpent and the Llama seemed to draw nearer. Then you asked them to speak to you and felt like an idiot, so you began to speak to them instead. You spoke to the stars in a voice that was quiet but fearless, and you told them things you'd never told anyone before. That you had a man's body, but wished you'd been born a woman, that you had dreamed several times about rubbing Old Gioconda's hump, and how once you'd pissed on Esther's taffeta curtains.

All of a sudden, the horse stopped and backed up. You patted its neck, flailed your bare feet against its cold torso, but it wouldn't move forwards. It kept backing away, rearing its head as though wanting to turn, but it only took small steps backwards, as if a wall were barring its path. You observed that the landscape had hardly changed, there was almost no tussock grass left, but the sound of water could be heard nearby, growing louder and softer, and a warm wind was arriving from somewhere, a wind that rocked you, waves with no sea.

The wind seemed to be coming from one of the rocks, one that was different from the rest, higher, with an opening to the east like a cave, and when you saw it, you felt ashamed at being there, in front of it, as if you were supposed to pay respect. Before that rock you lacked any desires; perhaps you had never felt this way before, so immersed in what you were looking at, as if your body ceased to exist on a slow night.

Calmly, you climbed down from the horse and then began walking extravagantly, without knowing why. You were almost dancing, swaying your body from side to side, your feet marking a rhythm that was unknown to you. Step backwards forwards two to the side, it seemed to be saying, step sideways forwards two steps back. A strange melody influenced your body without alerting your head. In this way, you approached that stone cave, that lap of the earth, and saw it was fenced off with tall, solid stakes. As you came into the presence of its broad darkness, you felt your legs sting; you hadn't even noticed the cuts you'd received as you moved between the rocks. You crossed the ring of stakes and your bones ached. Only then did you turn to see that the horse was no longer there, and you felt yourself orphaned of father, mother and animal: the most orphaned of all men.

But you continued to dance without knowing which

path to take. Within that darkness, you couldn't even be certain that there were paths. Then you remembered the oil lamp and your stiff fingers attempted to light it with a match, you struck the rock and a flame sparked up for just a moment to reveal the children of the earth. They were lying there, the ones who'd been missing, like fetuses, spreading their warmth. You managed to glimpse Berta, and Gioconda, and Tadeo, sleeping like animals. The flame burned out quickly, and then you thought of the plump fig-leaf gourds spat up by the vegetable gardens, with their umbilical stalks, and believed you were witnessing the same thing, bodies the earth nurtured with its sweet milk.

Without meaning to, you tripped over one of them and seemed to plunge into a pit; your body was no longer moving, but you continued to fall. A hand grasped you by the ankle and dragged you out. You knew it was him, the one you'd spent so long searching for. Your father dragged you like a stranger, an intruder.

Only once you were outside could you see beneath the starlight that it was true, that he had no hair, only a bald, shiny head and a large, beardless mouth; the folds of his skin were clean and his eyes gave the impression of being dusty, as though white, the eyes of a dove or a figurine of the Baby Jesus.

He emitted some sounds you were unable to understand. You showed him the palms of your hands, as they had instructed you to, as a sign you meant him no harm, and he touched your skin and face, like a blind man, and when you spoke, he tried to listen to your name, although it no longer seemed to hold any meaning for him. Víctor, you repeated, and he looked at you, tilting his head, now to one side, now the other. Víctor, your son, you said again. You touched his skin, which was new, smooth and shiny, a map, a primitive version of your father. You stood like that for a long time, feeling each other with your fingertips, tracing circles over those features that were two faces of a single being.

In that moment, you heard a gathering noise. As if the animals that lay beneath the earth were speaking to you, as if the forest were simply the herbaceous cult of a vast cemetery that was inhabited by more beasts than men, dead at the hands of man, nourishing the earth for man; they groaned, lowed, bellowed, an animal chorus that penetrated the soles of your feet and pierced your mind. Within that chorus you recognized the rhythm of your dance, the one that had led you to the cave, and began moving this time as if your body knew no other way than that delicate dance of the night.

Your father began to dance with you, imitating you, like in the mirror game. The night turned brighter and his movements seemed to invoke the Serpent and the Llama, finally speaking a language that was older than the word, the language of the stars and light, which caused the body to vibrate and disturbed the flesh.

Soon, other bodies began to emerge from the cave. They brought with them a warm wind and moved nimbly, possessed by some spell, their faces enraptured, eyes a milky white. You were not impressed by the breasts that dangled from the women but rather by all those shaven heads lit up by the moon, including Gioconda, who came out last, with a smooth skull and that deformed and bony hump where her spine mimicked a mountain range.

Even the living resuscitate, you thought, and you wanted to run back to the rest, to give them the good news. You would have liked to be able to tell them that the others had not gone missing, that they weren't planning anything wicked, that they'd simply been reborn, that you should all be happy for them and allow them to be free, and pray that one day the same might happen to all of you. You would have liked to be able to sing them the music you could hear in your ears, that funeral prayer of the animals that made you dance, pleasure of pleasures.

But at that moment, the charm wore off, and the faces of the children of the earth became deformed, their bodies stopped moving; all around you small whirlwinds formed, raising the dust, and on the other side of the cave a cacophony of voices both human and mortal grew louder. It was them, your people, Baltasar, Abdiel, Germán, Hermosina, Esther, coming with flaming torches, sweaty and riled up. The two groups came together and you had to choose.

So you did: it is always better to side with the dead. You took hold of one of the stakes that fenced off the cave. Death was a suffering filled with promise. You buried the stake in your chest. You gazed into your father's eyes, which were like the eyes of the horse, eyes of a specter, an animal. Within you, the song persisted, a howl. You sensed that your father was hearing the same thing, you saw him take hold of a stake. Finally, you were one. Only then did you know it was true: the Llama and the Serpent foretold of blood. And this was no bad thing. Far away, you could hear the howling of Agustina, Manzi and Filatelio, and you knew this was nothing but an answer to the wild animal chorus you had inside you, forbidden to men, who do not even remember the voices of their dead.

May the heavens and the earth curse you! you said to Abdiel, to Baltasar, to Esther, to all of them, without understanding why, and a trickle of warm blood rolled down your chest. In the beginning there was pain, but afterwards you felt that your body was no longer a burden, a torment, you were outside it, one with the tepid wind that surrounded you. You thought this was what death was, a return to a place that was so good, so mindless, so crazed, to where Cocuán did not exist, nor your mother, nor your brother. You locked eyes with your father; you had finally found each other, dancing, alone in the same game. And, at the end of the game, you both fell to your knees.

BALTASAR

Haven't you noticed the wind, kid? Now that everything's over, it's tepid and docile.

The weather's been changing. No one listened to me when I said it, but the wind was surging from the rocks, it came whooshing out, it blew inside us, shook the boughs of the trees. It was the wind that roared in our heads, that stirred up the pigs, the horses, the goats. It seemed they'd sprung up from the earth. They surrounded us, intimidating us with those bewildered eyes. And the birds, madre mía. We couldn't see them to begin with, but it was as if they were in every single tree, sharpening their beaks. Imagine hearing all this and understanding that, within the other, the person you have in front of you, there is a new man. Yes, kid, yes. It seemed as if they'd created themselves anew, with their own hands, that they'd covered themselves in a smooth new skin and placed transparent eyes in their sockets. Imagine that this other, who once was small and ugly, looks at you, and just by looking, he destroys you, pours salt inside you; and then, so great is the shame, because you're dark there, because you always have been, because you'll still be you, small and ugly, that you want to tear out their eyes to stop that look from burning you. Then you understand that the other has seen God or the devil, that he's seen something you haven't, and that he's no longer like the rest of you, of flesh and bone: he's discovered he has a fountain inside him and he splashes there, brimming with glory.

And this other looks at you, bringing you face-to-face with his shining scalp, because that's how they all went around, with their heads shaven, just like newborn babies, you saw them yourself. He looks at you, and you loathe him. And filled with loathing and empty of guilt as you are, you demand an answer from him, a word, something to prevent you from doing the thing you want to do. Because deep down it's as if someone were telling you, "Go on, do it, no one's watching." And none of them, kid, not a single one of them said a word. They didn't try to defend themselves, to explain. They were just this mute thing, as if they'd lost the power of speech. They were like animals, persecuting us with their silence.

Put your hands on my ribs, guambrito, the air's leaking out of me. I'm suffocating. That's it, that's it, you're very kind.

It all started with the wind, I tell you, the wind raged and the crag seemed to spin around us. We'd arrived there ready to grab them by the hair and drag them back to Cocuán. I don't remember how we reached that place, we followed the noise, the wind that blew harder in that direction. Nor did we expect to have to force them to come back with us. But too many things had happened in between. Return plans always turn into tragedies. When I close my eyes, I see a carrousel in the forest that spins and spins, and when it comes to a halt, instead of horses, it's they who appear, on all fours; they look at me and howl. And their howling makes my temples throb. When our flesh throbs, kid, we become unsettled. That's why we're so afraid of them. Watching children run and sweat has always sickened me; it reminds me of how the heart can quicken, like when you mount a woman or kill an animal with your bare hands, that's when the stomach slackens and the blood courses around your body in seconds, you could do anything in those moments, all the things that don't require thinking, you could leap onto a roof, fold yourself in half, because your brain isn't working and nothing else exists but the throbbing of your red and bloody meat, and flesh is wicked, kid, it makes you want to devour the other. That's why the old women in Cocuán always kept themselves covered up, and why young girls were forbidden from working up a sweat, running, becoming fresh and tempting meat. God himself created us this way, with thick blood and rotten flesh; but the others seemed to possess a new blood inside them, made from red earth and cosmic dust. The things the ancients said we carried inside us—or what it's claimed they said, because no one ever saw the ancients. It's only voices that talk, that whisper in our ear, it's only the wind, just like this tepid wind. Maybe we weren't born all in one breath, but in a roar.

I'm tired, kid, so tired. I'm not even sure what story I'm telling you, everything's fragmented inside me and it all arrives impregnated with black air, like the stuff inside my chest that's suffocating me. All on account of that foolish woman, pouncing on top of me, she was like a flaming torch, pursuing me. But I'm confusing you, that happened much later. It's enough to make you laugh, the way everything went down, laugh until you're out of breath.

In the beginning, the first ones to die were Old Jonás and the boy, his son, the taller one, yes. I can never remember his name. He had a bruised face, his knees bent too much when he walked and his hip jutted out, as though poorly positioned, like a doddery old lady, the kind who fall and bust their hip. No, that's not right. They bust their hip and then they fall. It's a small crunch no one hears, a crunch deep inside, as if the crack went snap and then laughed, ha. Jonás was on the ground, his face looking up at the sky, saliva mixed with blood dribbling from his mouth. Show some courage, ass-licker, I wanted to tell him. But his son was staring at me, the tall one, yes, I already told you, the one who walked like an old lady. He had his eyes wide open, his legs out behind him, his back on top of his legs. It was a strange position to be dying in, but the thing is, he was already dead. He was staring at me dead. The rest went to check if there were any more wounded. They went round and round those rocks. I kept watch over the others, who by that point had fallen back, cowed by our fire, by the torches that lit up their bald heads, and had gone to hide inside a cave. I watched them out of the corner of my eye, unable to look away from Jonás. I saw how he died. It's strange to contemplate death, kid. It doesn't leave you scared, just cold. While the others walked in circles around the rocks, I went over to him and removed his gold crowns. He didn't scream, mute just like the rest of them, he merely looked up at me with those white eyes of an old dog, while I tugged at the crowns with my trembling hands. I got no more than three crowns, because Jonás was a greedy old man who preferred his alcohol. This wouldn't cover even half the money I'd loaned them, not the original sum nor my interest. It didn't matter, though, it was some form of compensation, I didn't know what was coming either, I still thought we'd be returning to Cocuán, fewer of us, perhaps, but we'd return.

Then María and Ezequiel appeared, the stragglers. By the time they showed up, by the time they were standing in front of me, I'd already hidden the crowns in my pocket and Jonás was writhing. There's nothing we can do, I told them, and the boy laughed. María threw herself on top of Jonás. She didn't even see her other son, her dead son, she just hurled herself on top of that stubborn drunk, still in his death throes. Ezequiel grasped her by the underarms and pulled her up. Quiet, mamá, quiet, he said. And then he gave his father a kick to the head, followed by another and another, that's how he finished the old man off, while his mother tried to stop him, crying and half out of her mind. Ezequiel was the other son. He no longer seemed pained by that blow to his head, his eyes gleamed and his hands were shaking, like a maniac. And when Jonás stopped breathing, he crouched down, whispered something in his ear, then spat on him and began leaping about like a monkey at the fair. I couldn't hear what he said, I didn't want to either, I'm not some old busybody, and the boy seemed sick in the head. I fingered the crowns in my pocket and asked God for this all to be over quickly.

If you would give me a little water now, I could tell you what happened next. A few drops will suffice. Come on, guambrito, I remember you well. I used to give you alms when I visited the monastery. That whole beating thing earlier was because you were putting us all on edge, don't hold it against me like that.

Well, okay, it doesn't matter, just the water will do.

I was created with such indifference, I can't even die right.

Say, if I finish telling you this story, will you put me out of my misery?

Then I'll carry on.

Listen closely. Once Jonás was dead, Abdiel and Germán went after the others. Yes, that definitely came later. We left Jonás and his son, both quite dead, with María crying over them on the ground. Abdiel and Germán headed toward the cave and forced the others out. That cave was a dark thing, full of echoes. They were dazed, fearful. They made us chase them. I don't know what was going through their heads, they looked back at us from another world. Lucía was at the front of the group. She charged off—they all tried to, but she was more agile, racing toward the highest rock. Abdiel went after her, hot on her heels. Germán stayed behind, keeping the others penned in down below. Lucía was looking everywhere with those discolored eyes. Abdiel got so close he could breathe in her ear, and she panted, she looked like a fawn, trembling with fear. Fear of her own husband, kid, as if she didn't recognize him. It was like chasing a pack of savages. Lucía could do nothing but back away in terror. Until the rock called to the abyss. She was cornered. We believed Abdiel was going to catch her, was going to bring her down from there. He tried to take her by the hands. He got down on his knees, begging her to remember who she was, because that's how it seemed, as if she couldn't remember a thing. Who'd ever seen him beg before, but he was begging.

Lucía stared at him for a long time, moving her head like a deer, from side to side, I tell you they were like animals. Then she began to move back, back. She took a false step and fell.

She was dead before she hit the ground, I swear, from sheer fright.

After Jonás and his son, next was Lucía, daughter of One-Eyed Jara and María Catalina, the girl who could summon mist with her voice. That's what they said about Lucía, because when she hollered at night, it was said we'd wake up surrounded, buried up to our knees in mist.

When her body touched the ground, I heard the beaks of all the birds inside my head, like a hundred knifegrinders in a single room. The others were stunned, they surrounded her and began to snarl and moan, they were yelling something, but it was impossible to understand them. Then I saw them, the things I could hear inside me. A load of turtledoves and swallows appeared, flying low. They swooped, crop-first, all around us. Their wings wounded us and their squawking became unbearable.

It was all a shock. The birds pecked at us, gradually damaging our skin. Tadeo, Gioconda and Berta seemed desperate, staring at the dead woman. Abdiel came down, pushed past them and stood before the body of his wife. He stayed that way for some time, not moving or saying anything. Germán went to talk to him, approaching him slowly. When he touched his shoulder, Abdiel tried to scream, but his voice wouldn't come out. It wouldn't come out, kid. He'd lost it. It had died on him. It was enough to make you laugh, I tell you. He waved his arms, desperate, touched his throat, it seemed he wanted to strangle himself. Germán tried to bring him to his senses with a smack, and Abdiel just sat down on the ground, mouth open and drooling. We left him there, beside his dead wife.

Do you hear that?

Do you hear it, kid?

It's the wind again. It stops and starts back up. Wounded animal. From a tempest to a breeze. A breath one moment, a hurricane the next. I've never felt anything like it. If I tell you the whole truth, do you think you could spare me a bit more water? Don't look at me that way, guambrito. Give me some water, I won't bother you much longer. Don't press so hard there …

Then the wind blew like a giant, small swirls rose up from the earth and roared. That's when the goats, horses and pigs appeared. The goats were climbing up the walls of the crag, balancing, approaching cautiously. The pigs grunted, and the horses arrived with their heads bowed, going around in circles, deranged, ataxic. They appeared from who knows where, from the earth, the rocks, from the minds of those people, the ones who'd turned into savages and now went around inventing nightmares for us.

We all stood there, watching, all of us, because by then Ezequiel and María had joined us. We were afraid of being separated. But Carmen took no notice. She ran over to Tadeo. She put her arms around his neck, kissed his eyelids and danced with him, as though he were a stuffed dummy, because Tadeo simply let himself be moved while he tried to push her away. And she refused to let go, clinging to his naked body, like some tramp. And Germán, of course, went crazy over his daughter. Just a girl. He tried to catch her, but she was already gone, her flesh seething. Flesh that desires is wicked. She didn't want to be separated from Tadeo and shrieked hoarse shrieks; she shrieked and clawed at the rocks with her nails as Germán tried to drag her back over to where we were. Her grunting mixed with the sound of the pigs and the bleating of the goats and the horses' hooves pounding arrhythmically against the stone. Carmen kicked and kicked, whimpering and screaming until Germán did what he had to: he cracked her over the head with a rock. Tadeo didn't even look at her, focused as he was on Lucía, as if we were nothing.

After Lucía, it was Carmen, daughter of Germán and the departed Laura.

We didn't weep or scream. Having bashed Carmen's head in, Germán wiped his hands on his pants and looked at us with the face of a moron, of a man who had killed his wife and, instead of crying, was worrying about where to hide the body. No one knew what to do. To be there was to shit yourself completely, to spill your guts, not from fear, or from sorrow, but like a baby that shits itself and then goes about its business, dropping things from a height just to see if they will smash. The animals watched us with those eyes that never meet your gaze. The pigs began rubbing themselves against the grass and rocks, and the horses carried on like fools, shaking their heads. The goats arched their backs to give birth—and I can assure you that they weren't even pregnant, but they arched their backs and began bleating and bleating, pushing as though giving birth. It was air they birthed. Bad air. Because a foul odor began to spread with the wind, a tainted odor. And the goats arched themselves even more, it seemed their spines were one the verge of bursting through their backs, and the birds hopped everywhere. And then Germán began to roar with laughter.

He laughed and he cried.

He cried and he laughed.

Listen, I told the others, it's the wind. Do you hear the wind? The animals started snorting, I'm telling you, they were snorting and moaning. No one paid me any mind and I began yelling at the goats and at the pigs to make them go—git, git—and then the horses surrounded me, staring at me in an attempt to drive me mad, I swear that's what they wanted. My temples throbbed, I could still hear the commotion of the birds inside my head. And that wind that came and went, blasting us in the face with that acrid stench, then going off to howl among the grass and bushes, which had thinned out, it seeming now that we were surrounded by nothing but rocks. As though inside a tomb. We had nothing but fear, kid, and we wanted something to remove some of that fear.

I'll say one thing for fear: it brings you closer to God.

The animals weren't afraid, and neither were the others.

But we were.

To the fear, we responded, Unto the ages of ages, amen.

Are you scared too, kid? Fear is an old man in sandals who fondles children while everyone else is praying. If you want, I can continue, I'll tell you everything, but first do something for me. Bury this. Yes, it's the crowns. Dig a hole over there. And wherever you bury them, bury me there afterwards.

We all agreed to go see them in the cave and then

leave that place once and for all, get away from that wind, take them back to town with us, willingly or not; there'd be time to bring them to their senses later. But María was trembling and pacing back and forth. She didn't want to go and would be no help to us, she was unhinged. It was impossible to explain things to her. She'd always been that way. It's why she always fought with Jonás, who used to knock her around to calm her down. She reminded me of my mother.

My mother gave birth to me, then went off to howl at the mountains. Papá had her chained to the fence, piss and shit piling up beneath her. There was no way of getting through to her, and with María it was the same. Esther gave her a couple of slaps and she didn't react, just ran off. Others followed—Mercedes, Chabuca and Zaida—and sat there sobbing with her while we got down to business.

Esther, Hermosina, Germán, Ezequiel and I went to see the beasts in the cave, kicking the pigs and goats aside while Ezequiel spooked the horses with the torch, coming close to setting one alight. We were sure that, the moment we grabbed them, it would all be over and we could return to Cocuán, as ancient peoples had so often done after God commanded everything be destroyed; and around the town, we would build a new one, a small town that would give rise to many descendants, and God would have us live for hundreds of years until we could see the fruit of our labor, and no one would remember those men and women who had run naked to the crag, fleeing from us, nor would they remember what we had done, what we would do to them for running from the future, from themselves and from our old town, which, nevertheless, was still our town, our homeland, the place where we lived and sinned and taught our hearts to beat slowly, fearing God, because God loves all those lost towns where he wields all the power, and God appreciates small towns like ours, kid, like Cocuán, where men feel chosen, and there's nothing better than feeling yourself chosen by God and heeding his call.

That's how we advanced upon the cave, feeling chosen, commanded by God, with the sole idea of putting an end to the sin they represented, so removed from everything, so naked and crazy. What we planned to do was not a sin. We needed to capture them and take them back to their homes, alive or dead, we couldn't leave them running wild out there, we had to open their eyes. We stepped trembling into the blackness of that cave, smelling their naked bodies and crouching down like children playing hide and seek. When we got close, we felt their warmth, we encircled them, sensing their living flesh, tender, their corrupted breathing, hoarse moans, and not a word. The fear grew and their silence was animal.

Ezequiel drove them like sheep, thwacking them with a stick and holding the torch aloft, as though herding them. That's how we brought them into the light. Now wrenched from the dark womb of their cave, they were little more than fawns. We tied them up. Yes, kid, we bound their hands and feet with my belt, with Germán's, with our sweaters, and we sat them down on the grass, back-to-back. Old Gioconda's hump was left sticking up, a deformed thing. The birds pecked at us, making our work more difficult, but we left them tightly bound, near Lucía's body, until we could decide what to do with them. By then,

Abdiel was no longer with us, he merely bellowed and drooled, clutching at his throat. We tied him up too, just in case. The animals formed a ring around them, as though standing guard, those damned animals that wouldn't leave us in peace. We already had too many crazy people, maybe it was contagious, maybe there was something in the wind that provoked defects in us, we didn't know, but we absolutely needed it to stop. We came together to make some decisions, and the noise grew, we couldn't think. Ezequiel wouldn't stop shouting at them, circling them and thwacking them with the stick, yelling that he was a magnificent boy, you'll soon see, he was saying, that the world is magnificent. And the pigs grunted, and the bewildered goats butted him with their snouts.

María appeared from who knows where, screaming at her son that if he carried on hitting those people, there'd be no saving him; he grabbed her by the shoulders and shook her, fixing her with those crazed eyes of his, then she ran over to see about untying them. The rest weren't with her. Where are they? What have you done with my daughter? asked Esther. But María just got on with it, crying and screaming as she tried to untie them, moaning like a madwoman. Esther shook her as you shake a child, until her head began to loll, her neck limp. The girls and Mercedes had gone. María said nothing more. I want you to remember this clearly, kid. They escaped from the crag, escaped alive. Wherever they are, that will be the future of our town. Wherever they've gone, they'll know what they saw.

It wasn't yet sunrise and there was no moon to give us light, only the stars that shone very nearby, as if falling. The fear grew, and with it, a radiance, a light that seemed to come from the earth. While Germán and Hermosina were struggling to get the others tied back up again, a flame lit up the darkness. An aura grew behind the rocks, in the still of night.

Ezequiel appeared and, skipping between the rocks, he set the others alight with his torch.

Everything started to burn.

The goats failed to notice, continuing to bleat as the fire singed their hooves; the pigs had their eyes closed, remaining still, as if enjoying the flames; the horses ran around in circles like a carrousel, faster and faster, and the birds rose into the sky with the smoke, an infernal vortex.

In that moment, I thought we might already be dead and inhabiting the hell of some maniacal god. What hell will we go to, kid? The one of the ancients or the one we were taught? The hell of the Indians or of the fallen angel? I'm dim-witted and slow, kid, and I'm tired. And right now, I feel I'd prefer to go to the animal hell that existed before our mothers, that place with a deer and no more humans, not like the one the priests speak of. Just like the language you gain without meaning to, heaven and hell are most likely the same.

Tell me, kid, do you believe in your mother's hell? All of us in Cocuán knew who your mother was. We also knew she was cursed. She drove Santamaría mad and would have driven the rest of us mad if we hadn't locked her away. It wasn't wickedness. But we didn't deserve all this, kid, or maybe we deserved it too much. Which amounts to the same.

The background, the sky, the rocks. Everything was white and even brighter than the stars. It was me, being invaded by light. That's the last thing I remember. The whiteness. The light. And I was dark inside, I always have been. I was born trapped by the night when my mother delivered me and ran off howling in the mountains. Perhaps we're all born howling, and it's by forgetting this that we condemn ourselves. Now I'm talking nonsense, kid. I'm running out of breath.

The white crag, the mind so white. Where was all that light coming from? I didn't know. But by the time I saw the colors of the earth again, everything was almost over. The strong wind fed the blaze. By then all of them, all the missing, were dead, the animals were charging about, burning, and a ball of flame was coming towards me. There was no trace of the rest of them, not Esther, not Germán; I imagine they were burning too. But a live flame was pursuing me while ashes rose into the sky like rain coming up from the ground, a black rain, deathly, enraged at God and the devil because neither had saved our town, saved Cocuán; then I saw that the flame pursuing me was none other than Hermosina, with her stout body and those skinny legs, filling me with a smoke that was killing me.

And I couldn't run anymore, I was already half-dead.

Finish me off once and for all, kid, and bury me near my crowns, then put a cross over me and piss on it. I no longer care.

HERMOSINA

I burned like an ageing sun. I burst through the air, arms flailing, in the grip of some sort of tantrum, for I was no longer so much a woman as a body, a thing that smarted and burned. The tingling in my fingers gave way to other sensations I dare not mention. And then I understood that I had previously been not a body, but a dish, a bowl, a hollow thing that, for better or worse, was now being filled with fire and soot.

Our mamita would always repeat the same psalm to us:

"We have heard with our ears, O God; our ancestors have told us, what you did in their days, in days long ago. With your hand you drove out the nations and planted our ancestors."

One night at the monastery, our parish priest, Father Santamaría, began to howl. On the next day, the chickens laid black eggs, the cows refused to be milked, bird droppings rained down on us, and I swear by our mamita that when we tried to speak, we howled too.

When we were children, Esther tried to drown herself. Esther was slim and, when they saw her, grown men would almost impregnate her with their eyes. She began dating one who came from the north to extract stone from the mountains. One day, he failed to return. Esther didn't drown herself, but her belly filled up with fresh water, living water. Esther gave birth alone in the fields. Our mamita never wanted to even look at her granddaughter.

In the background of my terror, a girl runs in flames with the heart of a guinea pig and the bleeding head of a bald priest.

The sheen of Baltasar's hair, his large bristly hands, the silver buckle of his belt. One day our eyes meet, one day he leads me up into the mountain and says, Sweetheart, let me do it to you, sweetheart.

It's the veranillo del niño. The wind shakes the corn-cobs, a fluff in the air that makes me think of good things, beautiful things: cooing to a child with chubby hands, a golden field in which to spin to your heart's content.

I spun around and my skin turned to spirals, flakes of popcorn, charred black. I wanted to tell Esther she was still beautiful, that I loved her. I made her burn. The first thing I took was her hair, like a handful of dry grass; it burned and her eyes turned into black holes.

It was during a veranillo del niño that I began to bleed and our mamita told me I would suffer, that there's no animal that bleeds for so many days and doesn't die.

From the psalm, our mamita would repeat to us:

"It was not by their sword that they won the land, nor did their arm bring them victory; it was your right hand, your arm, and the light of your face, for you loved them."

That's when Cocuán awoke full of steaming piss. Everything reeked, and they blamed the dogs. The church was dappled with small yellow puddles. It made you want to splash through them in your rubber boots and cover the whole world in urine.

Our mamita cried a lot when she noticed Esther's

tummy getting big. Big and round as a ball, for it was to be a girl. With her toothless mouth, our mamita would say, God ish jusht and will kill me fursht. She was ashamed of us. And the fact is, she had given birth to three women, which was like saying she had given birth to three doves, three starfish, oh I don't know— three useless animals.

When the others went missing, Esther said God was acting justly, that he had finally freed us of that scum.

Returning to the psalm:

"You sold your people for a pittance."

Esther was clever and slim. Esther was what men wanted. When I was small, I would stick woolen socks down my top, wishing to be what men wanted, and then look at myself in the mirror with those deformed breasts of poorly positioned socks, my parts becoming warm. Rotten, defiled.

To begin with, just small fires everywhere, scorched plains, the animals stepping through the ashes—them stepping through the flames. My eyes were burning. I tripped on the rocks, trod on a goat's tail, fell onto my backside, my clumsy legs in a tangle. I was burning by mistake, but how well I burned. I grabbed at the fire with both hands because it alleviated me, because it was hot, because that's exactly how it was, like turning rotten all in one go. Like being on a bonfire with a thousand faceless men.

Mercedes wasn't as close a sister to me as Esther. I'd seen Esther's nipples, they were small and pale, like a girl's, I would sometimes call out to her at night when our mamita shut me in the pantry till I stopped crying, and she would waft a burning palo santo around me and say it was to scare off men with evil spirits.

Is God being just when he allows men to do disgusting things to women?

The psalm:

"But now you have rejected and humbled us; you no longer go out with our armies."

A stone-hard heart doesn't burn. My heart allowed itself to be penetrated by light. Burning is the quickest way of ascending to the heavens. The wind stirred all I was becoming. It was black smoke rescuing space, light that illuminated the shadows of the night.

Who could look upon my face of light?

Who could look upon it?

Only God would be able to.

Only God.

The pigs also showed up at the monastery. One morning, they were all wandering about over there, grunting. They toppled Saint Catherine of Siena and Saint Dominic de Guzmán. During the night, we sacrificed them. Father Santamaría took charge, but we did not eat of their flesh, for it was unclean.

Baltasar pawing me everywhere, skin that burns and sweats. Baltasar with the silver buckle in his hand. Baltasar uttering a name that wasn't mine.

The day Esther returned with Zaida in her arms, our mamita refused to open the door to her. Go live with the one who took that thing from inside you, she said. But Agustina didn't allow anyone in her home.

I was suffocating and wanted to spin around, adore the fire and turn until I caught up with the world. The world turns, and if it stops, it dies. Just like when I was a girl, and my father gripped me by the underarms and everything would spin around without stopping, until he set me down and my insides twisted and I vomited. I turned and turned, and as the fire extinguished, I felt sorry.

Inside our house, at the back, beside the painting of the last supper, the ever-open Bible, always with the same psalm:

"Would not God have discovered it, since he knows the secrets of the heart? Yet for your sake we face death all day long; we are considered as sheep to be slaughtered."

These are my childhood memories: father playing the guitar at mass every Sunday. Esther, Mercedes and I looking at father and our mamita, who in turn look at Father Santamaría, over at our house because he has discovered us baptizing a guinea pig in church. Father kills the guinea pig. Our mamita imposes a punishment on us: a hundred Hail Maries in the morning and we have to clean the sacristy. The priest spying on us as we clean. Father Santamaría panting alone in the confessional. Mercedes goes mute. Then Mercedes speaks again, only to say, He's been looking for my soul for quite some time.

During the veranillo del niño, we would host novena. Everyone in Cocuán would come over to our house. Our mamita would switch on the living room lights, remove the sheets from the armchairs, bring the Baby Jesus out for a stroll and embrace him, bring the Baby Jesus out and rock him. When I asked if I could hold the little creature, she said, Hands off, wretch, he'll burn if you touch him.

I say, Yes, I don't mind, he can do it again, I'll let him do it to me on bended knee. He bound my breasts because he didn't like them like an old woman's, made me put on the faded white panties of a little girl.

Baltasar, sweetheart, I'll let you do it to me, I'll let you do it.

I was vibrant and menacing. With an oh, oh, oh, they tried to avoid my touch, my torch-body. I wanted more fire, and those who were with me burned. Now this one, now that one. And the goats charged about dementedly, assisting me in the task, and the pigs rejoiced, wallowing in the purifying flames. Then Ezequiel joined in the firestorm, with his little ragdoll face and a mouth that resembled a hole as he screamed, I'm a magnificent boy!

Germán burned impassively.

The church in Cocuán was decorated with flowers, honeysuckles and black-eyed Susan vines hanging from the lintels. Father Santamaría tore them down, already very angry and suspicious of us all.

Before Father Santamaría arrived, we would keep guinea pigs under our beds, and in the morning they came padding into the kitchen to huddle around the fire. He forbade us from keeping guinea pigs; he extinguished the fire in every home.

Papá never lifted me by the underarms again.

Father Santamaría had arrived, the Lamb of God who took away the sin of the world.

Baltasar handled his dick until it discharged a white milk. Outside of me.

Mildred was the sin of the world.

During the veranillo del niño, we took Mildred from her home.

Defiled.

Esther became round and flat at the poles, like the Earth in school books. She was no longer the woman who men wanted.

Mercedes went silent until Chabuca was born.

I am the fire of God that takes away the cold of the world.

In the background of my salvation, a girl runs in flames with the heart of a guinea pig and the bleeding head of a bald priest.

She screams and screams, always the same psalm:

"We are brought down to the dust; our bodies cling to the ground."

And when flesh becomes fire, I try to reach you. Baltasar, sweetheart, don't run. It's all over now. Flesh that burns rises like cosmic dust.

We are alone and I burn.

FILATELIO

The fire rises and falls. Rises and falls. I told the fire we were leaving now, not to pester us with its noise. The rocks are cold and there is only night and, within that night, black pigs covered in ash make sounds like little ferrets and leave, charging and tumbling down the crag. Baltasar says nothing more, not a peep, he's been swallowed by the black air. He was a talking corpse and now he's a silent corpse. The rest are ashes the wind carries back and forth, back and forth.

We start walking, quickly. There's mist and droplets of rain that get inside your sweater, spreading cold everywhere and spilling over your brains, where the fog settles and makes your jaws creak. We must move fast, tearing through the forest with great strides, wheezing. Diosmadre awaits us on the other side. Slope after slope and then a lake. That's where Diosmadre lies. There will be great celebrations when we reach her, and we, the chosen, will provoke swirls of rose petals and thrushes will come settle on our heads. The sun of the wind will arrive early every day and hide itself just as early. All of this I was told by the heart of Diosmadre, when it gave its last beat. Yet she is neither alive nor dead. Diosmadre is the silt in which sows wallow and also the chorus madwomen hear when they sleep peacefully.

We move as swiftly as we can. We're watched by rheas from the wild heart of the forest, poppies sprout in our wake and, occasionally, spirits tread on our heels. The first encounter of those we left at the crag is with the forest, now their spirits flee like a weak and crippled chick does from the rest, because failing to do so would result in cannibalism. Other souls will also try to devour our dead, because they are new arrivals, outsiders on those plains they will now never leave. Even in death there are those who live in exile. They come and go and come and go and never adapt, because in death they smell of turpentine, of fake forest.

We stay close to one another, as if we've grown used to it from so much time spent this way, with our backs pressed together, around the qishuar, the way we were left by those who are now all dead and gone. For a long time, we told each other stories. Agustina said, Birds shit when they're happy. Manzi said, Our lord shat. I told them I had a secret, but they already knew, so we howled. And the rest left us there when they went to the crag—git, they said, stay over there. And it's a good thing they did, because we're as foolish as a box of frogs. We think of Cocuán and the most we can see is a table, a fly and a chair. It's important that the wood creaks and the rapid buzzing of the fly punctuates our foolishness. The chair should have four legs on which a dog pisses night after night. The fool sits there, before the empty table, with the fly attracting and maddening him in equal measure. With his less clumsy hand, he strokes the dog and beholds the face of God. That's how it is with us fools, but more often than not, we outlive the rest. This is because, as children, they push us in the dirt; we aren't like the others, small and fearful. Don't speak to him, he's a fool, they all say, so the fool grows up speaking to himself, thinking too much, about light and what he imagines to be fires up in the sky and the song of the cicadas. At the monastery, no one talked to me, only Diosmadre, until her heart stopped.

In the beginning was Diosmadre, and her womb that was rotten with me.

Now Diosmadre is as silent as a louse and is the sin of all men.

The grace of Diosmadre is preserved in honey.

She wears the dress that is the sky blue of the veranillo del niño.

It would be easy for us to become lost now the foxes have closed their eyes, the thrushes have dropped three times into a sleep of poppy petals, the night has rained down and Cocuán is still so far away. But Agustina has the gift of clairvoyance. In the time we've been away from Cocuán, she says, three hundred and seventeen pigeons have been born and a whole colony of wasps has died. Seven men and seven women have also died. In the jungle, three wise men looked for oracles, singing to the light. The stars have been burning, yet no one has noticed because of the mist. The mist endures. The mist is eternal.

Manzi shakes his head, as though it were full of birds, and screams. I touch the places where his ears once were and he gives a start. Manzi hears things I cannot and moans, Living flesh is wicked, living flesh is very wicked. So are black hens, I tell him, which lay eyes instead of eggs. Tender owls' eyes: devoid of face and carcass. Wicked too are those women who do not bleed, women who do not moan when the hand of a saint squeezes their breasts, two lumps of pink and broken flesh. They do not believe it. Blood won't save them either. There are women who bleed too much and beget children with the word coagulated.

They call us tontos, fools.

Father Santamaría, who knew Latin, said that tonto comes from attonitus, to be left dazed after a loud noise or commotion. Perhaps we fools are the only ones who hear our own cry when we are born.

Then we hear nothing more.

Nor was I a fat and rosy child. Poor. Disheveled. I was a prophet, just like my mother, and like all lunatics who talk too much and roam freely, like wild pigs, rolling around in the hay. I roamed the monastery at odd hours, kissing the hands of Diosmadre and painting the walls with the truth about flesh.

Señor Santamaría, you will die before the festival of San Juan.

It was his red and fat-cheeked face that made me laugh. He locked me in a fusty old confessional. The confessional is a resonance chamber, you open your mouth and spit out a sin that echoes in the head of the priest, and then at night it burns him. The priest draws it out gently like a fragile object he'll never share with anyone, he cares for it, waters it, and once it has become a great big sin that can walk on its own two feet, he lies down with it, he caresses it a lot, that's for sure, it's big and meaty and can last him for days.

It doesn't matter that it's dark, the night gives us the jitters, sprigs of rue that blossom inside us as we continue to walk towards the waterfall. Now is when we discard our rags and go down to the water where nobody knows us, and Agustina leaps about and laughs, she trills like a turtledove. Manzi doesn't enter the water, he sits stone-still upon the donkey. He lives like that, sleeps like that.

Agustina gets out and, naked, curls up among the nettles and honeysuckles, red splotches appearing on her skin, and she presses herself down into the green. I follow her, and we spend a good while looking up at the stars.

I brought you into this world, she says, your mother screamed and cried her eyes out all night long. She already knew she was finished.

Diosmadre has never died, I respond.

Her hips were so narrow you arrived covering your face with your hands, as though ashamed at being born. The skin of her tummy split open.

Who sent for you?

Santamaría. We all heard how your mother used to scream in the night. I put curses on that priest. I conspired to make his dick fall off.

He kept it in formaldehyde and looked at it every day, I tell her, it was his personal god.

Santamaría had no god.

Diosmadre is my god.

Manzi's howl informs us we must carry on, and we proceed naked, our skin covered in welts. Manzi goes to touch his ears and smiles, hearing nothing, he is very close to light, which is as deaf as a doddery old lady, then he says, Blessed are those who have not seen God, for they shall inherit Orion's belt, the constellations of the Llama and the Serpent, and the fire of the stars.

On high, an eagle screeches. Why? It is drunk with forest.

Midnight comes and goes; now the moon illuminates Manzi's old bald head and the flowers of the black-eyed Susan vine open in its radiance. There are no stars, only a sweet mist, like that which got into the eyes of those who left. Deep white waters, like in the minds of fools who breed perch they will never be able to fish.

For you, for you, for you, Diosmadre, we will cross centuries of pines.

They also disparage the forest, stealing water from the earth. In Cocuán, men dirtied your water, Diosmadre, they sanctified your river, which was not made to be sacred but to be unhinged by the word. The coagulated word is a word of Diosmadre, the dirty word, brooded over, the word of the fool that is composed of blood and shit. The time of Diosmadre is not sacred, it is the common tongue that a god tore up from the earth, a dead and forgotten tongue. We are naked and alone. I grumble, Diosmadre, it burns me. Agustina skips, Manzi carries the silence forwards. What will become of us? Three sad fools. When the sun begins to rise, we rest our heads against a root, the large root of a diminutive tree; tired, we stop to pee, like brooding hens, all three of us squatting down. It has started to rain and we continue walking. From here we can already see Cocuán.

We hear the barking of the dogs.

It is raining so heavily we can almost see how the honeysuckles and jasmines grow around us, how they tangle across the path, in spirals, and all is green, white and green. The rain pelts down, and the grass pursues us, becoming taller and taller. We break into a quicker pace, stirred by what we are seeing. Cocuán, with its half-finished and empty adobe houses. Cocuán, with its streets of dirt, mud and stones. The broken streetlamps, around which galaxies of moths and flies circle, the stench of drink and drains stinging our noses. There's another smell we struggle to identify. It's a smell of flesh, of cow pats, of thick pig's hide and bird piss, a smell of the unhinged. Near the monastery, the animals gather and the sound is wild and barbarous, they grunt and groan and beat against the door with their snouts. The street leads us down, then back up again. Cocuán rises and falls, rises and falls. There are no faces in the windows, only the flapping of white birds that have installed themselves on tables, in kitchens and in bedrooms. The donkey brays and Manzi flinches on top of it. We sink into the crackle of the animals and advance silently, almost without meaning to, toward the door of the monastery, where something glows.

Behind it is Diosmadre.

Everything has ended in Cocuán.

Here were born the men who would kill her.

Here too the women who smelled her sex.

It smells of buttermilk, they said.

Her skin sheds like the damned, they sang.

In Cocuán, they have killed God's daughter.

Yet God does not know.

No one has told him.

Nor does God know that hares are witches, that black hens devour men, or that Agustina hides pagan spells within her words. Just now, she has managed to pacify all the animals, the goats, pigs, horses and dogs. May the mist be of your eyes, she told them, may the whiteness fill you. They all listened and rested their front legs on the ground. Now they lie at the feet of Diosmadre and the dogs lick her hands and spin, going round and round in circles. As it always should have been. There is no light in the monastery, and we don't need it because Diosmadre's body glows. She has been left skinless, a complete angel, an apparition in living flesh. Living flesh is. Wicked the children of Eve, wicked the hands of man from the very start, wicked the beasts and wicked the dreams in which they appear, wicked the visions of women, and wicked the children they do not bear, wicked the words that have not been wrought by God, wicked the bitter cold and wicked too the mouth that kisses the flame.

Diosmadre does not get up, she has not revived, her dead body remaining warm for an eternity. Father Santamaría had wished to burn it and sink it to the bottom of the river. It's not like she was a saint, she didn't work miracles. Santamaría turned to drink and saw that it was good and pleasant, and yet it could not make him forget, so he tried to devour the flesh of Diosmadre. Not even this could save him from madness. Santamaría penetrating God, Santamaría hallucinating about a god who could save him from all that earth and flesh. Santamaría condemned, a dead man among so many living, with the word made pus. His sermons reeked. Word of God, we praise you, Lord. And the body of Diosmadre remained intact, skinless and pure.

You don't have to be good, Diosmadre's eyes told me.

You don't have to whimper or cry, they pleaded.

Diosmadre embraced the exiled children of Eve.

And there I was, accursed fruit of her womb. Before her I prostrated myself at all times. Every day and morning I would kiss her hands, recite tainted prayers to her. Until I understood that it was time to leave, because men had become confused and gone off with white eyes. Diosmadre told me this with the purest wind. She told me the night had come when people vanish in their places, she told me the fire rises and falls, rises and falls, and that fire rules in the mountains.

Now we return to you, Diosmadre.

And our laughter crashes against the belfry and grows.

We take her body in our hands. A body full of light. Men cannot look upon it. The animals surround us, now the black pigs grunt and wallow, the goats do arched jumps, and the dogs leap up and stand on two legs to sniff her. The mist and a strange dawn wind enter through the door and caress us. The wind is tepid, it settles on our heads and makes us howl.

We take Diosmadre to her river. And, as we walk, no one looks at us. The salvation of Diosmadre will not be history. And the daughters of Cocuán will remember what they saw, because Mercedes, Zaida and Chabuca live on, and yet wherever they go, no one will believe them, because Cocuán does not appear on any map and it is only among ourselves that we murmur of the time when Diosmadre reigned on earth. No one will listen to us. Don't listen to him, he's a fool.

The body of Diosmadre is not weightless. We carry it between the three of us and Agustina stops from time to time to catch her beath, while Manzi shakes his head full of birds and screams. We are followed by the pigs, the goats, the dogs, several white horses, a deer that hides among the rest and bleats, and a hare that appears and disappears, appears and disappears. And when we reach the river behind the house of Diosmadre, we observe each other in silence and release her body into the water.

The river sparkles, as if the stars were beneath it, a liquid firmament.

Then Agustina and I enter the water. In our pockets we carry the ashes of the dead, which settle over the silence of stones and sediment. Here lies Baltasar, here Carmen and Tadeo, here Ezequiel, Víctor and María, Jonás, Germán, Gioconda, Berta, Hermosina and Esther, here Abdiel and Lucía. To the water we return the misbegotten children who God has stolen from it. Here lie the people of Diosmadre, who vanished one night. Forever and ever.

And then, instead of a juniper tree, we take shelter beneath a quishuar and listen to the wind, that tepid wind, the wind that causes the waters to recede, the wind that brings turtledoves and swallows. And nothing has transpired in the world, except that Diosmadre has vanished in the way all gods vanish in one place or another.

A trail of light that sinks until nothing is left, only the murmur of fools and an animal song no one on Earth can hear.

[Author bio TK]

Book Club Discussion Guides on our website.

World Editions promotes voices from around the globe by publishing books from many different countries and languages in English translation. Through our work, we aim to enhance dialogue between cultures, foster new connections, and open doors which may otherwise have remained closed.

Also available from World Editions:

On the Isle of Antioch
Amin Maalouf
Translated by Natasha Lehrer
"A beguiling, lyrical work of speculative fiction by
a writer of international importance."
—*Kirkus Reviews*, *Starred Review*

About People
Juli Zeh
Translated by Alta L. Price
A novel about the social and very private consequences
of the pandemic, written by Germany's #1 bestselling
author Juli Zeh.

Fowl Eulogies
Lucie Rico
Translated by Daria Chernysheva
"Disturbing, compelling, and heartbreaking."
—CYNAN JONES, author of *The Dig*

My Mother Says
Stine Pilgaard
Translated by Hunter Simpson
"A hilarious queer break-up story."
—OLGA RAVN, author of *The Employees*

We Are Light
Gerda Blees
Translated by Michele Hutchison
"Beautiful, soulful, rich, and relevant."
—*Libris Literature Prize*

On the Design

As book design is an integral part of the reading experience, we would like to acknowledge the work of those who shaped the form in which the story is housed.

Tessa van der Waals (Netherlands) is responsible for the cover design, cover typography, and art direction of all World Editions books. She works in the internationally renowned tradition of Dutch Design. Her bright and powerful visual aesthetic maintains a harmony between image and typography, and captures the unique atmosphere of each book. She works closely with internationally celebrated photographers, artists, and letter designers. Her work has frequently been awarded prizes for Best Dutch Book Design.

Euan Monaghan (United Kingdom) is responsible for the typography and careful interior book design.

The text on the inside covers and the press quotes are set in Circular, designed by Laurenz Brunner (Switzerland) and published by Swiss type foundry Lineto.

All World Editions books are set in the typeface Dolly, specifically designed for book typography. Dolly creates a warm page image perfect for an enjoyable reading experience. This typeface is designed by Underware, a European collective formed by Bas Jacobs (Netherlands), Akiem Helmling (Germany), and Sami Kortemäki (Finland). Underware are also the creators of the World Editions logo, which meets the design requirement that "a strong shape can always be drawn with a toe in the sand."

www.ingramcontent.com/pod-product-compliance
Ingram Content Group UK Ltd.
Pitfield, Milton Keynes, MK11 3LW, UK
UKHW010846270625
460105UK00004B/80